FROG MOON

FROG MOON

Lola Lemire Tostevin

CORMORANT
BOOKS

Published with the assistance of the Canada Council and the Ontario Arts Council.

Edited by Gena K. Gorrell.

Cover illustration by Paul Perras.
Cover design by Artcetera Graphics, Dunvegan, Ontario.

Author photo by Jerry Tostevin.

Published by   Cormorant Books Inc.
                      RR 1, Dunvegan
                      Ontario, Canada K0C 1J0

Printed and bound in Canada.

Canadian Cataloguing in Publicaton Data
Tostevin, Lola Lemire
        Frog moon
ISBN 0-920953-61-1
        I. Title.
PS8589 .06758F76 1994   C813' .54   C94-900011-6
PR9199 .3.T68F76 1994

*For
my parents
and
my children*

CONTENTS

... the Moon is a desert. ... From this arid sphere every discourse and every poem sets forth; and every journey through forests, battles, treasures, banquets, bedchambers, brings us back here, to the centre of an empty horizon.

Italo Calvino
The Castle of Crossed Destinies

If we had a keen vision and feeling of all ordinary human life, it would be like hearing the grass grow and the squirrel's heart beat, and we should die of that roar which lies on the other side of silence.

George Eliot
Middlemarch

THE CHORUS (i)

One of the first things she agreed to when she arrived at the *pensionnat* was to join the choir. She wouldn't have dared join on her own but when Mère Supérieure showed her the auditorium where the concerts and celebrations took place and asked if she would be part of the choir she felt she had no choice. Besides, she loves singing. The first time she attends choir practice she throws herself into it with a fervour that would make any Mère proud.

"Singing is an extension of speech," Soeur Bernard tells the group of girls, pointing her baton to their chests and throats. "The secret to singing is the ability to imagine pitches and sounds and reproduce them from within." Soeur's open hand thumps her own chest and clutches at her breast as if to extract all the pitches and sounds harboured there.

She blows a high note on a small flute. "Now imagine this sound. What does it look like?" Soeur closes her eyes and from the look on her face it is clearly bliss she wants the girls to imagine; like the ecstasy in the picture of St. Theresa and the angel in the sacristy.

"Singing is affected by the clarity of the singer's mental image of what she wants to produce," she explains.

"You must imagine the sound."

The ability to concentrate on images has never been a problem for the young girl but imagining sound is another matter. What does sound look like? Soeur's visions must extend to reading minds for no sooner has the young girl finished wondering what it looks like than Soeur is standing within a few inches, blowing notes into her right ear.

"Can you reproduce these notes?" she insists.

What does wailing look like? The young girl tries to visualize the shrill note of the flute. Her mouth opens. *Caw. Caw.* Not exactly what she had imagined but hopefully close enough to Soeur's expectations.

"No, no. You are way off key and your voice is much too thin. You are not breathing," she warns as she taps the young girl's chest with her baton. "For volume you must breathe. Here, listen carefully, then sing these words while I accompany you on the flute." She hands the girl a sheet of paper bearing words between blocks of dots and lines.

The name of the song is "L'hirondelle". From the swallows that nest under the eaves of her parents' garage, she knows swallows don't sing. They chirp and twitter. Still, concentrating on the sound of the flute, she imagines the long slender wings and forked tails of adult swallows sweeping towards their mud nest. The hungry beaks of chicks receiving their daily ration of mosquitoes. She moulds her mouth to the vowels on the page as they form in the back of her throat while her tongue forges consonants in her own beak mouth. There is, she knows, a sound that will penetrate to the heart of these words, mould itself to the stump tongue of a swallow. The Chinese, she's read somewhere, received their musical scale from a bird called a sing-sing, and maybe it will now come to her rescue.

Tap. Tap. Tap. "Perhaps," Soeur admonishes, "it is not always enough to imagine. Perhaps one must also have been blessed with a musical ear. "You," she says, pointing the end of her baton towards the young girl, "do not seem to have been blessed with any ear at all. For today you should just listen. Just follow the music and practise the words by mouthing them, as if you were reading to yourself."

For the rest of choir practice, then the next, and all the choir practices that year, the young girl will stand in her assigned place among the other girls and simply mouth the words offered to her on sheets of music. For weeks, months, a year, she will attend choir practice without ever reproducing one note, at least not out loud. Three times a week she will stand in her usual place in the third row and mouth the words the other girls sing, her own song suspended in mid-air as if its story had escaped. Sister will forget about her, or simply accept that faith alone can't always move mountains or cure a tone-deaf girl.

Only God could be at the heart of such fervour. Deaf to her own voice, the young girl mouths words of songs with such zeal it's as if she were bearing news directly from heaven. But gradually, like a cloister releasing its latch, new vistas begin to unfold in her head. With each choir practice, each concert, her silence gives way to something other than God. Each silent word gives way to an image, the image the word would have stood for.

As she articulates each vowel and consonant against the roof of her mouth or her lip, as if reading to herself, each letter spirals into the shape of the object it is about to spell. Each letter of each word twists itself into an image like the decorated letters of medieval texts she discovered in the convent library. The letter "f" grows into fish, into flower or frog, each letter carving the empty space of her mouth into a familiar shape. If the choir is singing about birds, aviaries flutter from her throat. Worlds made even more vivid by their absence.

Once, during the Christmas concert, while she sings "Mon beau sapin", her silence fills the auditorium with a forest of northern pines, fresh snow, and the aroma of her mother's *tourtières*. And several times while she mouths her favourite song, "La lune éclaire", a luminous moon, round as a glyph, spills from the young girl's mouth and fills the entire room.

BABEL NOËL (i)

Last night, on our way to a Christmas concert, Christine and I saw wicker furniture on sale in the window of a fashionable furniture store; the same mossy green as the settee and the matching chair my mother had put in the cottage when I was a child. Heirloom wicker, the clerk called it when we enquired, but it wasn't wicker. It had the same intricate patterns, and the coated steel and aluminum frame made the lace grid more durable than natural wicker, the clerk said but it would never bear the outline of three generations of bodies. *Wickersham* Christine called it, the two of us dissolving into giggles like the two convent girls we'd once been. It had been a long time since I'd thought of Madame Wickersham.

It had been a long time since I'd been in a church as well. The concert was held at Holy Trinity. Not that it's still a church—its use is relegated mainly to concerts and plays nowadays, as if religion had finally admitted it had never been more than an art. Nor was it a choir of women as when Christine and I were *pensionnaires*—at least, not exclusively, it never is any more. Voices in the night. The meditative murmur of nuns chanting nocturnes or matin lauds just before wake-up call, the first stirring to give thanks for the light that has caused the night to pass away. And almost every night as we drifted to sleep, the same voices singing vespers, giving thanks for a night of rest from the labours of day.

We've always kept in touch, Christine and I, although we only see each other once or twice a year now. She divides her time between Toronto and Paris, her necessary exile she calls it, and I do envy her her artist's life. Doing exactly what she said she would always do, especially after Madame started to lend us all those books. The Brontës, George Eliot, Virginia Woolf.

The children love it when Christine visits, she exemplifies everything that I'm not; her artist's worldliness, clothes with just the right bohemian touch, her Parisian accent. Louise never misses an opportunity to flaunt her French School French, especially in front of David, but mostly it's the stories about when the two of us were friends at the *pensionnat* that they want to hear. Christine keeps insisting, as she always does, that I got into more trouble than she did, and as usual I protest, but Louise and David like to believe it's true.

"Did Mom really have to carry a roll of toilet paper for an entire week because she wet her bed?" Louise asks, pressing for details, delighted at the thought of her own mother wetting the bed.

"What did Mom write on the blackboard that time the nun asked her to specify the main characteristics of a vowel?" This is one of David's favourites and Christine is more than willing to oblige. I suspect she takes great pleasure in reminding me, via the children, that I wasn't always this lacklustre model of domesticity and motherhood.

"You mean the time she wrote that the *bowel* is the

most prominent sound of a syllable," Christine tells them for the umpteenth time. "Your mother must have stayed in the corner for two hours that time. She was quite the rebel, always sitting in corners with cards blazoned in red hanging from her neck: *J'obéirai la règle du silence pendant la période d'étude; je ne parlerai pas dans la sainte chapelle; je ne répondrai pas aux chères soeurs lorsqu'elles me réprimandent.* Humiliation tames the spirit and elevates the soul, the nuns always said."

"Is it true the nuns would put their hands in front of the movie projector if the actors kissed?" the children grill Christine, as if to confirm what I've already told them several times—coming from their mother, it must be too peculiar for them to accommodate. It's easier to accept the pact these stories offer from someone else, someone they only see for a few hours once or twice a year.

"They were always obstructing the projector. If actors kissed or if the leading lady's *décolleté* was too low. The main thing I remember about The Great Caruso is the shape of a hand over the screen when Caruso kissed Ann Blyth. It was okay to kiss a leper but it was a sin to see Ann Blyth kissing Mario Lanza."

"Kiss a leper! Gross! Why would anyone do that?"

Kiss a leper. If a sinner became a missionary in a leper colony and kissed a leper her salvation was guaranteed. Like kissing the wounds of Christ to purify one's soul or something as perverse as that. Encouraged by the children's reaction, Christine related how I had announced to my parents one Christmas that I was planning to join an order of missionary nuns in China, so it wouldn't be necessary to buy me presents that year, and Louise and David were beside themselves trying to imagine their mother a nun in China.

J'obéirai la règle du silence. The words sprang from a moment I thought time had erased. Words rooted in marrow. The *pensionnaires* more manageable when not allowed to speak. Weeks, months, carved in silence. That's probably why I love listening to ourselves talk, even if we do repeat the same stories over and over again. They give shape to those long expanses that would have been forgotten otherwise, each story as intimate as family or an old friend. That's the way it is with stories. You come to appreciate them for their good intentions, aware that they don't always tell the truth. They shape people, towns, landscapes, and cheat you into believing certain things about yourself. They select, discard, and amend plots that become history. That's how we invent ourselves.

The rose-coloured bracts I've placed around the fireplace are the same colour as the vestments the priest wore after weeks of austere purple. Advent marked a time of hope and promise as each girl counted the days until she would be going home for the Christmas holidays. *Veni, veni,* rejoiced the antiphonies in the chapel as they intoned the Magnificat, their voices carried higher and higher by the gladness of a pipe organ and bells. I don't know why I chose the pink flowers this year instead of the red. When we returned from the concert Christine referred to them as *poinsettie* and, as close as that is to its English counterpart, it didn't draw the same feeling as poinsettia, which is normally red.

As Christine left last night she commented on the impeccable state of the house, undoubtedly a condescending remark since house cleaning has never been one of her priorities. Nor is it one of mine, I explained, but my parents were coming the next day for the holidays. I didn't admit that I'd been scrutinizing every nook and cranny for at least a week. My mother always assesses a woman's worth by her floors. "Her house is so clean you could eat off the floor," she declares after visiting a deserving acquaintance, so I always make sure that she can eat off any surface of the house, if that's what she wishes.

Not that she ever comes right out and says that the house isn't what it should be, she's much more subtle than that, so I never really have anything tangible with which to confront her. Except once when I caught her remaking the children's beds, muttering to herself that it was impossible to keep a bedroom looking half-decent with those fancy new comforters young people used nowadays. The softness of duvets doesn't measure up to the sharp corners of tucked sheets and blankets of convents' or mothers' beds. If, at the time, I felt justified in telling her she had no business in my children's bedrooms, the guilt and tension that pervaded the rest of the visit made the fleeting satisfaction not worthwhile. Middle-aged and still my mother's child.

The clamour from the upstairs hallway is too familiar, the predatory tones of children arguing. I doubt they have straightened the second floor as I asked. Since David has been at university since September, his room is in fair shape, but Louise's notion of tidiness isn't even near mine, let alone her grandmother's.

"*Louise. . . . David!*" I shout their names in as French an accent as possible, partly as a reminder that their grandparents will be here in a few hours but also because they know that I often revert to French when exasperated. As if some emotions can only be expressed in the language closest to those emotions. As if fragments of myself can only link to specific sounds. An argument Geoffrey and I were having recently disintegrated when we both realized

I was hurling French at him while he was yelling back in English. As if some emotions had to defy the barriers of one language in search of closer bonds. As if living in a language that is not your mother tongue cuts you off from memory.

Geoffrey and I made certain that the names we chose for the children couldn't be altered significantly from one language to another. As trivial as it may seem, changing only one letter of a name can make one feel cut off from a source. My mother often calls me *ma belle*. *Ma belle rebelle* or *ma pauvre Laure* she says, while Geoffrey always calls me Laura. *Une poinsettie*, a poinsettia. The child who spoke French is no longer the adult who speaks English. She is the smallest doll in a set of nested dolls like the one Christine bought for Louise in a Russian gift shop, each doll living within another version of herself, as in a vault.

It isn't that I don't look forward to my parents' visit; except for the two years Geoffrey and I spent in Paris with the children, the family has always spent Christmas together, and now that they are growing older it's even more crucial that we do. It's just that since I've been teaching, there's no time for rituals, as if tradition had become external to the demands of everyday life. The presents, the shopping, the cleaning, the cajoling, the food. It was so much easier when the children were small and all we had to do was buy a few toys and look forward to the usual excesses at Grandma's and Grandpa's. My mother's life doesn't revolve only around keeping a fastidious house, she is also a remarkable cook. While I resent the hours chained to a kitchen stove in the name of tradition, my mother revels in it. "*On n'engraisse pas les cochons à l'eau claire*, she says as she ties the strings of her apron behind her back. It wouldn't be Christmas without her.

I'll have to remind the children again to make a special effort to speak a little French this visit, a token. Louise will protest that she doesn't understand her grandparents' accent, that it's not the way she learned to speak French at Toronto French School, and that Grandma thinks she's a snob when she speaks that way. Why can't we all speak like Christine, she'll say. David, on the other hand, will reassert that he intends to stick to English and "if people don't like it they can lump it." Once again I'll find myself making excuses for the children. I must seem so foreign to them at times. They will never experience how parents come to life again when, after a long absence, I hear them speak their mother tongue. I sometimes feel as if I don't belong to either my children or my parents. During those moments, when the mirrors of both languages crumble, I have the unsettling impression that I will always remain a stranger to myself.

"*David*, don't you think your gym and hockey equipment should go in the basement?"

"It's too cold to work out in the basement, Mom!"

"And I suppose it's too cold to play hockey down there as well. In the basement, David. Let's get it done, your grandparents will probably be early as usual."

"When are we going to decorate the tree?"

"After dinner. They like to help."

"Are we having *tourtières*?"

"We're making them tomorrow, for Christmas Eve."

"I hope Grandma doesn't forget her pickles and chutney."

My mother takes weeks to prepare for this yearly ritual so she seldom forgets anything. The two of them will work their way through the shovelled artery from the garage to the back door looking like two magi, carrying themselves as if they had been invested with the supreme authority to oversee a tribe, hauling boxes of green pickles and red chutney, cookie tins, parcels bearing pictographs of pine trees, trumpets, and bells. My father will renew his threats that he's getting too old to drive the four hundred miles but everyone knows he's as committed to these rituals as any of us. Failing new values that can sustain his hopes and faith, it's as important to him as to all of us that we preserve a semblance of tradition at least once a year. The re-creation of a small part of history through which some degree of relevance is restored, if only for a few days.

Louise has retreated behind her bedroom door and a compact disc Christine brought her from Paris, undoubtedly hoping that I've forgotten all about her. When I open the door she complains that I invent needless chores, and in the name of women's rights she claims I expect more from her than from David, especially since I've been teaching. I point out that it would be somewhat impractical for David to come all the way home from university to clean her room and do her chores.

I should never have accepted a 9 a.m. class. But then, I would have agreed to anything, I was so grateful to have a job. Teaching anglophones how to write English in a university run by old boys. Things haven't changed much since Madame Wickersham. If it's true that on judgement day the elect will gather from the four corners of the earth, I have no doubt they'll all be male and they'll all be speaking English.

"Why don't you tuck your sheets under your duvet, your bed looks messy like that," I suggest from the doorway, trying to stay on the safe side of intrusion.

"Oh Mom, nobody cares what my bed looks like," she moans as she falls back on her bed in a gesture of exasperation.

"Grandma cares. She'll be in here remaking it if you don't."

"No, it's you who cares. Give it up, Mom, you're not in that stupid convent now."

GOLD DUST

The white iron beds with the white cotton covers are lined up in four rows, a night table separating each bed from the next. While curtains enclose the nuns' cells at each corner of the dormitory, the spaces the girls are assigned offer no privacy. Every night after prayers, *Je crois en Dieu le Père tout-puissant . . . ,* the girls kneel in front of their night tables and make small tents over their bodies with their dressing-gowns. *"De la pudeur, mes filles, de la pudeur et de la chasteté. Souvenez-vous que votre corps est un temple,"* the supervising nun reminds them as she marches up and down the aisles trying to spy any evidence of wanton immodesty.

Besides the risk of jeopardizing the sanctity of her bodily temple, the young girl also knows it's important not to expose any part of her body to the moonlight at the top of the dorm windows. That could turn her into a *loup-garou,* so she crouches as low as she can under the make-shift tent. She's heard of children who exposed themselves and grew long silken hair on their bodies, and slanting eyebrows that met on the bridge of the nose. "I pine for blood! Human blood! Give it to me and I am yours, body, heart, and soul," they moan when they wander the woods of Northern Ontario at night.

She removes her black stockings, the garter contraption the *pensionnaires* call their chastity belt, then her panties. Stooped almost to the floor, she pulls her black dress and her slip over her head. The girls who wear brassieres contort themselves to reach their hooks, although most girls in this dormitory don't wear them yet; by the time they do, in a few years, they'll have been transferred to the other dorm.

As each girl takes off a garment she neatly folds it and places it in the night table—except for the dress, which she drapes over the metal foot of the bed. She then retrieves a nightshirt from the night table and slips it over her head and shoulders as both hands push simultaneously through its arms and the arms of the dressing-gown tent. It's only a matter of weeks before each girl learns to complete this exercise within two minutes without compromising her sense of modesty.

The most difficult time for the young girl during the first few months at the *pensionnat* is when, immediately after going to bed, she hears, over the nuns' prayers in the chapel, the music from the skating rink at the parochial school just beyond the convent fence. "Skaters' Waltz". It begins in late October and the first time she hears the music, she imagines herself among other figures, her mother and father, her friends back home. This is the first time she conceives of herself as an image, the first time she visualizes everyone she cares for as a memory: her house, her school, the skating rink her father nurtures every winter in the backyard, the larger skating rink at the Protestant school a few blocks from the house. Her ankles are too thin and her skates turn in too much for her to be a good skater; nevertheless she loves skating, has loved it ever since she received her first pair of skates for Christmas when she was six years old. She's already outgrown her second pair and in her last letter home she asked for figure skates for next Christmas.

The snow, transient specks drifting past the dorm windows, is silver here, which isn't the case everywhere. In geography class, Soeur said that the snow in Greenland is often green and sometimes even red, but here, in the silver belt of Northern Ontario, the snow is silver. Unlike Timmins, where the snow is gold. Because of the gold dust, her mother said. It's so luminous and blinding that it looks white but it's really gold.

In the beginning, when the sun spun its rays around Northern Ontario, its filaments burned everything it touched, turning everything to gold. That's why there's so much gold in Timmins, her mother said, so much of the land is rock, so much of it lined with long gold threads. Often, when her father came home from drilling the gold-ore veins that course through the rock at the Hollinger mine, gold dust clung to his overalls, and her mother turned the cuffs inside out looking for particles concealed there. The particles were barely large enough for the eye to see, but after she'd run the tip of her index finger along the inside crease it bore a faint mist of light.

It's because of the gold dust that the fields and roadsides around Timmins are covered with buttercups, her mother said, as she placed the yellow flower under her daughter's chin to see if her daughter liked butter. It's because of the gold dust that in spring goldenrod wields its wands all over this northern land, and covers it in goldweed so that there's a haze around the gold-dust tree. It's because of the gold dust that the goldwinged woodpecker calls everyone "flicker . . . flicker . . . " and it's because of the gold dust that the goose lays golden eggs.

Gold dust settled everywhere. The Golden Trail, Golden City, Val d'Or, everything acquiring its gilt-lettered name, marigolds, goldfish, *oreille, orteil. Tu es de l'or en barre, ma belle*, her mother said, making her more precious than anything or anyone else. At the Golden Dragon restaurant in North Bay, half an hour from the *pensionnat*, she filled up on egg rolls, chicken fried rice, then asked for chop suey to delay having to leave her parents as long as she could. She had to be in before seven o'clock, *l'heure du dragon*, she called it.

When she first saw the wall around the *pensionnat* she was reminded of the Wall of China. She had read about the Wall in her mother's *L'encyclopédie de la jeunesse*. How the evil emperor who had built it had also burned the books of his empire to protect himself and his subjects from undue influence. She even had tea occasionally with the more honourable emperor who lived in the Palace of the Moon, and who sought to save the empire from the unscrupulous emperor.

Whenever she had tea with the emperor, she dashed around placing cups before her dolls and poured perfumed liquid into blue porcelain cups no larger than apricots. Each person drank slowly, according to the ritual, holding the liquid at the root of the tongue as long as possible to let its savour penetrate before making its way to the heart.

"This is unlike any tea I have ever tasted," the young girl would exclaim.

"That is because this *tch'a* can't be found anywhere else, not even in the garden of the palace," the emperor would reply. "It grows amid ancient rocks and its needles are finer than the pine needles of your country. In the winter my servants gather the needles on the snow on the

Holy Mountain, place them in jars that have sand at the bottom, and turn the jars towards the east to gather the sun's rays. The jars are kept like this for months while the sun imbues the needles with the purest aroma known to anyone. When the time comes to make *tch'a*, water is poured into an earthenware pot and boiled on a fire made of dry branches. If you listen to its song you will hear the wind beckoning through the pine boughs." Into a red teapot at least sixty years old, the young girl poured the boiling water over the pine needles and, on special occasions, an orchid, and while she let the *t'cha* brew she performed the dance of the umbrellas or the butterflies, her voice mewing like a lute or a violin.

At the emperor's invitation she sometimes attended elaborate banquets in the room of the yellow storks, and while they ate the marrow from the bones of a phoenix and the tongue of a bird called sing-sing, she always requested that the emperor tell her a story. *Kaki s'inclina devant l'empereur en signe de respect et, les yeux brillants de curiosité, interrogea son hôte généreux: 'Puis-je connaître votre histoire, mon empereur?* In the voice of the emperor she made up stories in her own gibberish, then exclaimed, *Quel beau langage, qu'est le Chinois!* and the emperor would tell her how wonderfully she spoke it.

She wished she could write to her mother in Chinese so Soeur wouldn't be able to read their letters. She wished she had a brush with an ivory handle and bristles made of hare fur. She would dip the brush into sepia ink and with her wrist moving like the wind the ink would fall like gold dust, as she drew pictures as graceful as a dragon's flight or a serpent's dance.

The designs she would draw, the words she would invent, would be as fluent as when gold marries jade.

Instead of *bonjour maman* she would draw a sun above the horizon. For "I miss you when I go to bed at night" she would make an outline of a heart and a moon in the same sky; the phrase "I want to ask you if I can please stay home after Christmas" would be depicted by a mouth that filled the doorway of their house. And at the end of the letter, to warn her parents not to forget their only daughter, she would draw a divided heart with her mother and father on one side and herself on the other. After decorating the margins with flowers and vines, she would fold the sheet in the shape of a bird and send it floating all the way home.

As she drifts to sleep, the moon on one eyelid, the sun on the other, and skaters waltzing in her head, the young girl remembers the angel with the gold-tipped fingers. On the night you were born an angel placed an index and a thumb on either side of your face and gave you dimples. A child with dimples is marked for life, her mother said.

FROG MOON

My first memory is of my mother telling stories.

"By the time you were three months old you answered to the name of a frog." Not unusual for a French Canadian, except that my frog was Cree. Kaki. Shortened version of Oma-ka-ki, second creature born to Oma-mama, earth mother who birthed all spirits of the world.

Native men were getting good money working as diamond drillers in the gold mines so many of them were leaving the reserves with their families. When my mother became very ill when I was three months old, an Algonquin woman who lived in our neighbourhood helped her wean me, and she nicknamed me Kaki. Undoubtedly because we were French Canadian but also because I was born in the month of June, month of the Moon of the Frogs.

I often wondered what my mother meant when she said an Algonquin woman helped her wean me, but I never asked for details—preferring my own version, almost certain it wasn't the right one. There are some stories so factually accurate the names of the main characters have to be changed to protect the innocent, while there are others whose facts are so irrelevant only real names should be used.

Kaki. Short version of Oma-ka-ki, second child of Oma-ma-ma.

Cree legend has it that Oma-ma-ma's first-born was the powerful thunderbird Binay-sih, who protected all creatures of the earth from a mysterious and destructive sea serpent; her third-born was the famous trickster Wee-sa-kay-jac, who held the enviable power of transforming himself into any shape or form. He could often be seen in the shape of a small boy riding the back of his wolf brother Ma-heegun, fourth child of Oma-ma-ma's. I, on the other hand, was named after the croaking voice of the lowly frog, holding few magical powers except for the endless chore of controlling the insects of the world.

My first memory is of my father telling stories.

"When you were three years old you wandered from home one day, strayed away on your new tricycle. We lived near the Temagami River and by the time I came home from work in the afternoon the whole neighbourhood was frantic in its search."

According to the story, my father, before setting out and in a voice meek with embarrassment, turned to my mother and asked, "But what's her name?" Inside our house or with relatives and friends I was known as Kaki, but in front of strangers and within earshot of neighbours my father must have thought it inappropriate to call his daughter by a name that was not hers, a name associated with an element even less desirable than French Canadians. In the presence of strangers he felt compelled to call his lost daughter by a name she wouldn't recognize as her own. Kaki was not a proper name; that would be retrieved at the age of nine, when I was sent to the convent, when the time had come for me to be proper.

All my life I've had to move from one place to the next

but the names of childhood are where I continue to dwell. The Temagami River. Algonquin Boulevard in Timmins, until we moved to Iroquois Falls near Lake Abitibi, where, on Saturday afternoons, you could still hear the rumbles of angry Iroquois being led down the falls by an old woman from an enemy tribe.

Two or three times a year, to get to the *pensionnat* in Sturgeon Falls or, later, to the boarding school in Ottawa, we drove from Iroquois Falls through Mattagami, Gogama, Temiskaming, lunched at Lake Wanapitei or Powassan, drove on to Mattawa, Chippewa, Kanata. In my father's early-model Plymouth, my brown metal trunk full of crisp clothes in the back hatch, we travelled through a geography of foreign names that were no longer foreign. We remained unaware of their history while they coursed through our veins and became part of our geography, each line on the map a seam connecting us to something larger than we could grasp or understand. Maskinongé. Nipissing. These were the names from which I was weaned, their sound as sharp as wild berries on the tip of the tongue. That's where they carry their history as well as my own.

For the first few weeks at the *pensionnat* I never answered when someone called or asked my name. When I'd been christened I'd been given a name, and by virtue of that name I'd become a main character in the stories my mother and father told me. This was my family bond, the name I was to carry through the family album, except that at three months I was given another, as if my character had taken a small detour through some other plot. Kaki was not my name. I was not Cree. I was not a frog. Nor did I encounter any frogs for the first few months in the convent. None was ever mentioned in daily mass or in the books of prayers and meditation.

After a few months, as I got used to my real name, I forgot about frogs, until one day when Soeur came up behind me and exclaimed, "What was that you said? Was that a frog that came out of your mouth?"

Just as I'd been in the habit of hunting down English words in my dictionary at home, I began to hunt down frogs in the convent library to find out why they would be coming out of my mouth. I hunted them in dictionaries, encyclopedias, but my main source was the Bible. In the beginning was the Frog.

From the Book of Exodus they came pouring out of rivers into a place called Egypt; they invaded houses, bed-chambers, ovens, until millions gathered and died in heaps all over the land. From the Book of Psalms frogs overran the privacy of kings' chambers, while in the New Testament they emerged in the shape of foul spirits from the mouths of dragons and false prophets. Foul spirits was what Soeur meant. Frog was just another word for swearing, another dirty word.

Gradually, frogs took up residence everywhere. In English class, Lancelot, Galahad, Percival all frogs in shining armour, sat around Frog Arthur's table. In French history, Charlemagne's avenging of Roland became "Revenge of the Frogs". During reading period, sleeping frogs Gawain, Robin Hood, Don Quixote, Sancho, all waited for their princess kiss.

Study periods were often spent making up ditties. God is a Frog sitting in the fog at the bottom of the bog. Or making up biblical frog casts. Kings Og, Gog, and Magog became the Three Stooge frogs caught in perpetual western movie plots. Frog Gog led barbarian hordes against Israel but in retaliation the Israelites defeated Frog Og and recaptured the borders of their Promised Frog Land.

Years later, sitting in the wicker chair in the sunporch of my parents' cottage, reading Orwell's *Coming Up for Air*, I was delighted to read how the main character, George Bowling, had invented his own plots around the Bible's Og and Zog. As a young boy, while singing psalms in church, he had renamed Og and Zog Ogpu and Zogpu, and declared one of them the King of Lower Binfield, where he lived. Confined to riddles they can't relate to, children borrow from the fiction of other bodies, word-creatures, tricksters, and make them travel their own maps.

THE IRON HORSE

I rode the iron horse for the first time when we moved from Timmins to St-Bruno on the Quebec side of Lake Temiskaming, when I was seven years old. Everyone called the train the iron horse then because someone was supposed to have misunderstood *le chemin de fer* for *le cheval de fer*. Probably the English, my mother said. When it came to French, the English couldn't put three words together without getting one of them wrong. The English, the main prong in a French Canadian's three-pronged fork.

Whenever my mother told me how she brought her mother's body back to Cochrane on the train from Ottawa, I envisioned a black iron horse, eyes fierce as coals, nostrils smoking, prancing the tracks, clickety-clack, clickety-clack of hoofs on the railway tracks, and my grandmother's body in a wooden box. Clickety-clack, clickety-clack, break your grandma's back.

I don't know how many times I've heard how my grandmother worked herself to death and how that made her an angel. An angel was someone who had borne seven children by the time she was thirty-three, looked after them with next to nothing because her husband was only seventeen himself when he married. His father had taught him carpentry, he was a good cabinet-maker for his age, but after a day's work he assumed that he could go out at night, that it was his due. Drinking and "other things", my mother called it, adding furtiveness to the long list of components that went into the making of an angel, her voice resigned because that was what was expected in those days. An angel never complained, worked around the clock, and if she got tired, she went to Monsieur le Curé for guidance. The Clergy, the second prong in our three-pronged fork. I suspect that's why my mother had only one child. No man was going to tell her to bear a child every year, no man wearing a dress was going to tell her how to run her life. Clickety-clack.

    We moved from Timmins to live on my great-uncle's farm, *mon oncle* Ti-Roc, on my father's side. He was getting too old to look after things and he promised that my father would inherit the farm if we moved in and helped. We'd just had the phone installed two weeks before and it was as if the offer had come directly from heaven. As good as the money was, diamond drilling at the Hollinger mine, my father said it was too much like being buried alive. He'd come home covered in soot, black as a bug, and tell us about elevators crashing to the bottom of a shaft or dynamite detonating at the wrong time. Our neighbour had been killed in a cave-in and one of my uncles had almost died in a dynamite blast. He'd spent months in the hospital with so many bits of rock embedded in him, his body looked like a crater. For years he had specks of stone coming out of his skin and he would give me a penny for every fragment I could extract. Clickety-clack. All that frontier living was closing in, so my parents decided it was time to move on. They sold everything they owned in Timmins, their four-room house, the furniture, and we set out to sow our seeds of independence.

My father was very excited with what he found: acres of arable land, a large house, a rural setting on the edge of nowhere—in short, paradise. My mother, however, was wary from the beginning. Someone fibbed about snakes in paradise, she would tell friends and family later, "It's roosters that cause all the trouble in paradise, the way they rule over the entire coop," and *mon oncle* Ti-Roc's rooster was particularly vicious. It was my mother's job to feed the chickens but the rooster wouldn't let her near them. That's when she learned chickens weren't very smart. She tried leaving food on her side of the fence but they wouldn't walk around the fifteen feet of wire open at each end. It was quite a sight, my mother with a bucket of feed in one hand, a broom in the other, and the rooster prancing up and down, his comb cocked two inches on his head, daring anyone to cross the fence, and even if we didn't cross it he'd chase us all the way back to the house. Never stalked men, but hated women. I don't imagine he ever recovered all his feathers. My mother would just as soon have wrung his neck, turned him into a stew, because God knows we needed the food. The only thing he was good for was waking us at dawn every morning, he was an expert at that. Went off like an alarm when it was barely light, the signal for my mother to get up and prepare breakfast for the men, because they worked like horses and would have eaten like horses too if there had been enough food in the house.

We arrived in St-Bruno as I was entering grade two. My mother wanted me to make a good impression on my first day of school and she'd sewn me a brown woollen dress with a row of red apples and smocking across the front. Apples for the teacher and all. I was especially proud of my matching red socks and my red schoolbag. But when several children called on me to walk the new girl to school my mother broke into tears. She'd made a terrible mistake, she said, dressing me up as if we came from the city. The children were mostly in rags, one of them wasn't even wearing shoes, they were poorer than the poorest in our neighbourhood in Timmins. We'd been a little short at times, had taken clothes-hangers to the dry cleaners for a penny apiece, but we'd never wanted for anything as important as shoes. This was not what she'd planned for her daughter.

Poverty mustn't have been a concept I worried about because I don't remember how the children were dressed, but I do remember several of us going to the general store in *mon oncle* Ti-Roc's horse-drawn wagon after school. According to my mother, my uncle had the same temperament as his rooster, and just about as much money. He'd promised to buy whatever food we couldn't raise on the farm and my mother had given him a list of provisions she needed but all we brought back was flour, yeast, sugar, and baloney. He expected my mother to make everything, including her own bread. She'd spent the first week cleaning the farmhouse, scraping hardwood floors, slathering them with wax, buffing them by hand, had hardly complained, but she drew the line at having to make her own bread. "I've never shunned work, but your grandmother made her own bread, shined floors by hand, made our clothes, took in other people's ironing, bore a child every two years, and where did it get her?" Clickety-clack, clickety-clack, break your grandma's back.

There is a photograph of my mother standing in front of her grandfather's shop, Louis Séguin and Son— Sash and Door, the sign in English because that's where the business was, with the English, and you didn't want to offend them by flaunting your French. She is wearing a coat her mother has just made her. There was nothing my grandmother couldn't duplicate from a catalogue, and every spring and fall two of her four daughters received a new coat or dress. If the required material couldn't be purchased that season, coats were turned inside out, recut, details changed here and there, and presto, a new garment was produced. Spring coats were made into winter dresses, winter dresses that showed too much wear were cut up for appliqués or made into collars and buttons for coats, because frugality was another requirement for angelhood. "What did the mother moth say to her baby moth?" my mother would ask me, trying to get me to eat everything on my plate. *Si tu n'manges pas ta gabardine, tu n'auras pas de crêpe de chine.*

"I remember the day that picture was taken, the first time I wore that coat, marvelling at how rich we were," my mother repeats each time we look through the family albums. "We lived above the shop, the largest apartment I'd ever seen, except for those two-storey company houses the English lived in, in Iroquois Falls. Everything seemed fine until my mother and I went to Ottawa to consult a heart specialist, and the next thing I knew I was bringing her body back in a box and everything changed after that." Clickety-clack, clickety-clack. "I'm no angel like my mother," she adds, "but I'm no Rose Latulippe either."

For generations, French Canadian fathers, afraid their daughters will dishonour the family, have related various versions of the legend of Rose Latulippe. Woman and her demon's gifts, because the Devil always entered a family's affairs through the female side. The Devil, third prong in our three-pronged fork. "In this respect my family remained pretty faithful to tradition," my mother said. "These myths often covered up what was really going on, but we're not supposed to talk about that."

The widower Latulippe had only one daughter, a beautiful sixteen-year-old whom he adored. My mother, also sixteen when her mother died, was the oldest of three still living at home. While the widower Latulippe catered to his daughter's every wish, my grandfather, distraught with grief, drank and ran around even more than he had before my grandmother died. There were also rumours that he was stealing from his father's shop, and within a few months of my grandmother's death he left his father's business and moved to Timmins with the three children, into a "two-room shack barely fit for pigs, it didn't even have floors."

"Men were very good at pioneering, prospecting, trailblazing, and spending nights at the whorehouse up the hill, but children, that was woman's work, and if the little woman wasn't around it didn't get done," my mother said. "I should have been in school but like most French Canadians I'd not gone back after the elementary grades. There were no French high schools in Timmins or Cochrane, no French high schools in Ontario until 1969. If you'd attended *l'école séparée*, spoke French at home, you couldn't keep up in an English high school, so almost no one made it past grade eight unless they went to *un couvent* or *un collège*." Her ten-year-old sister was sent to a convent but at sixteen my mother was considered old enough to fend for herself. She cleaned house for a well-to-do family for a few weeks but the three sons wouldn't leave her alone. She tried living with her oldest sister and husband but he wouldn't keep his hands to himself either. My uncle could never be trusted around young girls when I was growing up but we're not supposed to talk about that either. Nor are we supposed to talk about my mother getting pregnant a few months after she met my father, and how they married when she was only seventeen.

"I can't tell you what I went through that first year my mother died. I can't tell you because that's not the kind of story you pass on to your child. All I can tell you is, my life changed as abruptly as Rose Latulippe's did when the widower Latulippe gave a party on the night of Mardi Gras. As if my mother's death had been the stroke of midnight that marks Ash Wednesday and Lent."

My mother almost never misses an opportunity to turn an event into an allegory. Allegories allow her to hint at things other than what is actually being said. Her memory becomes so absorbed by the ambiguities of her circuitous accounts that the facts can be altered any way she wants, because they are, after all, only incidental details of a story. Allegories allow her to express her differences, whether they be with my father or with her past, without having to clarify the circumstances. Repeating the legend of Rose Latulippe while dissociating herself from its main character allows her to warn me against, while differing from, the moral of the tale.

As hospitable as he was, Latulippe had warned his guests that on the exact stroke of midnight the merrymaking must stop. There was a storm of the Devil's making outside, a terrible wind hurling snow at the shutters of the widower's beautiful country house. Inside, everyone was having a wonderful time, especially Rose. She danced every dance with a different admirer, rather than with her fiancé, the man her father had picked to be her husband. She did stop once, though, towards eleven o'clock, when there was a fierce knocking at the door and Latulippe, after a brief hesitation, opened it. A young man stood before him, a dark silhouette against the whiteness behind. He asked politely if Latulippe would give him shelter since he had lost his way and, at Latulippe's invitation, he entered in a flurry of snow.

When the young man removed his fur-lined coat the guests were astonished at how handsome and elegant he was, dressed in black velvet and cream silk. He refused to part with his dark fur hat or black gloves, undoubtedly the whim of a *seigneur.* With utmost grace he apologized for having interrupted the party and begged the host and guests to carry on with their festivities. One guest, casting a glance through the window, exclaimed, *"Nom du ciel, quel beau cheval!"* Everyone was dumbfounded at the sight of the stranger's mount, black as night, eyes as fierce as glowing coals, without a trace of frost on his magnificent, gleaming coat. Latulippe invited the young *seigneur* to put his horse in the stable but he politely declined. Such small eccentricities in a *seigneur de la ville* only added to his charm. Everyone was anxious when the young man accepted a glass of spirits and suffered a slight convulsion as he swallowed the liquid; no one realized that Latulippe had been short of bottles and had poured some of the *whisky blanc* into a flask that had once held holy water.

The handsome young man kept asking Rose to dance, and she seemed unable to tear herself away from this stranger who danced as well as she did. During all this time her fiancé, bursting with rage, kept eyeing Rose with a look as blazing as that of the black charger at the door. Still, it didn't deter Rose from granting the new arrival each and every dance.

At the twelve strokes of midnight the master of the house requested that everyone cease the merrymaking immediately, since it was now Ash Wednesday. Rose made a move to disengage herself but her partner held her and begged to continue, if only for a few minutes more. They were having such a good time, why stop?

Of course, Rose couldn't stop, and the young couple continued to dance into Ash Wednesday while the fiddler played his infernal music as if driven by some mysterious power. Rose's little feet scarcely touched the floor. In her turnings and gyrations, she moved like a puppet—no longer subject to the laws of gravity, no longer subject to her father's dictates.

As her handsome partner drew her closer to him, he murmured in her ear that from now on she would be his, and Rose felt a painful prick in the palm of her hand. In panic she uttered a cry of despair and lost consciousness in the arms of the stranger.

Suddenly, to the astonishment of the guests, Rose's features turned ashen and her garments began to melt away, leaving her completely nude. Her handsome cavalier was also transformed. His face now looked like the mask of a demon, and with Rose in his arms he rushed out the door and made for his impatient steed.

No French Canadian legend is complete without an epic battle between Monsieur le Curé and the Devil. Every Mardi Gras, while his flock celebrated at the home of one of his parishioners, Monsieur le Curé shut himself in his study to pray for the sins his flock would undoubtedly commit. But this Mardi Gras, while kneeling at his *prie-dieu,* he saw a gruesome vision. His enemy was in the act of molesting a young woman lying naked in the snow.

Aroused by the cries of the curé, the sexton dressed and rushed downstairs. As he opened the door of the study Monsieur le Curé yelled: "Isidor, quickly, go to the stable and get the grey mare."

"What has happened, Monsieur le Curé? Is someone in danger of death?"

"Worse, my son, a soul is in danger of eternal damnation. Run to the stable, there's not a moment to lose."

When the horse was ready, Monsieur le Curé galloped towards Latulippe's house. The snow was no longer falling and from a distance he could discern something stirring in front of the illuminated house. He struck the mare hard with his heels and, since she also sensed that something dreadful was about to happen, she shot forward as fast as she could. It was not a minute too soon. As the horse and rider entered the road leading to the house, another mount came towards them in a cloud of smoke and snow.

Face to face, the old enemies confronted one another above the still and naked body of the young woman, but they were unequally armed—for Monsieur le Curé had brought his stole, and he threw it over Rose's body. A cloud of fire and smoke discharged from the enemy mount, pierced by a loud, raucous cry. When the cloud had dispersed, Rose lay stretched on a square of melted snow and burnt grass. The infernal rider had disappeared.

Monsieur le Curé bent over the young girl, took off his cape, and covered her with it. After blessing her and pronouncing some Latin words, he lifted her up in his arms and carried her to the house. With his broad shoulders he brushed aside the men and women who had witnessed Rose's shameful behaviour, made his way into the living room, and gently laid his charge on the sofa. He turned towards the girl's father, threw him a long look of disapproval, and disappeared into the night without his cloak.

Of course Rose had to pay the price for her indiscretion. One version claims she became a nun, another that she remained an old maid, while another says she was married off to her fiancé and bore at least a dozen children. "There's no doubt in my mind which of these punishment is worse, but I'm not another Rose Latulippe," my mother concludes each time she tells the story.

After only two weeks on the farm in St-Bruno, it was obvious, even to a seven-year-old, that things were not going as well as everyone had planned. The tension between my mother, my father, and my great-uncle was barely kept under control until the second Sunday, when all hell broke loose.

People had stared at us on the first Sunday we'd attended mass, but we'd assumed it was because we were strangers, new members of the congregation, or maybe because we were dressed differently from everyone else. My mother liked to dress up, and in St-Bruno, Sunday mass was the only occasion where she could wear something decent. It was an Indian summer day in late September and she wore a short-sleeved dress and a little makeup. She never overdid it—a little rouge and lipstick and a faint line of kohl on her upper eyelids. Her hair was very dark and a little colour on her face brought out the highlights, she said. She was twenty-four years old and very pretty.

I don't know how we came to sit in the first pew that Sunday but I remember everyone's eyes on us as we walked up the centre aisle, and they remained fixed on our backs throughout the first part of the mass, especially when Monsieur le Curé searched us out as he climbed the pulpit.

He had the same peculiar way of speaking as everyone else in St-Bruno. The community had been isolated for so long that it had retained the accent and vocabulary of the inhabitants who had settled in the region more than two hundred years before, which explains many of the expressions my father still uses.

"God took affectionate care when he created the body of a woman from Adam's rib," Monsieur le Curé began. "He took affectionate care because he had a special role in mind for the woman's body. Her body is a receptacle, a vessel for the sacred duty of motherhood, and as we all know, my dear parishioners, each woman's body is a symbol for the vessel that carried the Son of God. There is no greater honour than that.

"There are some women, however, who believe that this role is not good enough for them. Some women have the audacity to suggest, through their actions or their dress, that God didn't know his job well enough so they've decided they should help Him. They decide that in addition to being a sacred vessel for one of the most important functions of mankind, their bodies should also be adorned, painted, even exposed, because they imagine—no, my dear parishioners, they assume—that one of the body's main functions is to attract attention to itself. Yes, my dear parishioners, we have among us a Jezebel."

"I couldn't believe my ears," my mother would tell everyone in Timmins later. "I'd abandoned my home, spent the last two weeks working my fingers to the bone for a few baloney sandwiches, and here I was sitting in a dreary little church at the edge of nowhere, being called a Jezebel by some half-cocked lunatic in a cassock. I can't help it if I'm in good shape, which is hard to hide unless I wear a potato sack, but my dress didn't even have a cleavage, for God's sake. Women as vessels. Who the hell ever concocted that? You can be sure it wasn't a woman. Vassals would be more like it."

I don't suppose my mother noticed the glares, or even cared, as she stalked out in the middle of the sermon with me in tow and my father trying to keep up with us. He could stay if he wanted, she shouted when we got outside, but she and I were leaving St-Bruno on the next train. She packed our belongings and the next morning she stacked them on my uncle's wagon, the rooster chasing us out of the yard. The three of us left on the next iron horse for Timmins, my mother muttering that she was no angel but neither was she another Rose Latulippe. Clickety-clack, clickety-clack, break your grandma's back.

BABEL NOËL (ii)

J'ai tu eu d'la chance d'avoir eu de si belles filles! my father exclaims as he enters the house and embraces his daughter and granddaughter. *Et toé t'as pas fini de grandir, mon p'tit maudit anglais?* he adds, tussling David's hair.

Within seconds of relieving their grandparents of their "CARE packages", Louise and David are working their way through cookie tins in spite of their grandmother's protests. Everyone is shouting over everybody else, as if each person represented a different clan speaking its own peculiar dialect. Louise shouts in what she considers her superior French while her grandmother tries to accommodate everyone by switching back and forth from French to English; David, undaunted by a conversation in which his grandfather speaks mostly French, perseveres only in English.

"So, Grandpa, are you going to lay bets on the game tonight?"

"*Les* Maple Leafs? *Ah non! T'es pas pour gager sur ces* bums. They're losers! *Ils ont perdu les dix dernières parties. Ils n'ont même pas gagné contre les Canadiens cette année. Mon pauvre garçon,* I can't steal your money like that," he says, while placing his two dollars on the table, making sure that David does the same. *"Louise, garde ben cette fortune, c'est ton grand-pére qui va la gagner."*

Within an hour, my mother has solved the dinner menu and removed the meat from the freezer, and is peeling potatoes, the unbroken peels curling towards the sink. My father has manoeuvred the children into working on the Christmas tree before supper, making sure nothing will interfere with the hockey game at eight o'clock.

From the time I went to the *pensionnat* I never took part in decorating the tree. When I came home two or three days before Christmas, it would be waiting, adorned, the presents already underneath, and it was taken down only after I'd left. My first Christmas with Geoffrey I meticulously orchestrated all the details so that our Scotch pine would be identical to one I'd seen in a book in the convent library: a stylized effect of red balls, golden birds, and white lights that I repeated each year until the children started to add their own creations from nursery school and kindergarten. Styrofoam balls covered in iridescent stars and metallic ribbons still hang beside the red balls and the few birds that have survived the annual migration to the basement. The birds are as important as the styrofoam balls. They symbolize an instinct that allows creatures to adapt to new surroundings and, when the need arises, to return to old ones.

The women's interest in hockey is not nearly as fervent as the men's but we know better than to interfere with the viewing of a game, especially between the Maple Leafs and the Canadiens. My mother and I always join the men, as if the importance of the occasion dictates our presence. My mother only looks up from her knitting or darning now and then, while Louise, depending on her current mood, either disappears for the evening or feigns obsessive interest in every detail to mask her boredom. But our attention is never as unconditional as the men's, although I've been known to get as carried away as anyone else, especially at David's games. Geoffrey never lets me forget how rowdy I used to get when he played amateur hockey, rowdier than most, he says, and I must admit there are elements of the game I still enjoy. How a group can claim an area of space and achieve mastery of concerted action defending it. The precision of a small gesture, a hidden impulse made visible when strength and speed travel from wrist to stick a split second before the puck enters the net. The eloquent expression of that barely perceptible flick. But I seldom say anything about that. In the presence of an activity ruled by force, only force can be acknowledged. Since hockey creates such powerful bonds between the three men, it seems only reasonable for them to watch it without too much interference from the women.

* * *

When Geoffrey returns from his business trip on the afternoon of Christmas Eve he finds the kitchen transformed into a production line of *tourtières*. After a week of restaurants, he's grateful for the aroma of savoury and clove that greets him as he opens the door. *Sariette et clou.* His mouth waters at the sound of their names. He can hear his mother-in-law and Laura speaking French in the kitchen and he loves listening to them. He wishes Laura hadn't lost her accent when she speaks English, hadn't yielded to the English pronunciation of her name. Her accent was seductive, alien, when they first met. It was a condition of their love. Now she could pass for English.

During his trip he pictured the three of them, his daughter, wife, and mother-in-law, in the kitchen, carefully measuring flour, shaping pastry dough into balls, his mother-in-law's hands moving at flashing speed, much faster than his wife's or daughter's. He imagined her flattening each ball with her palm, then with a rolling pin; with light strokes she would roll out the pastry into a circle, moving from centre to edge. When she'd reached the desired thickness, she'd coil the pastry onto the rolling pin, place it over the pie plate, uncoil it from the roller pressing against the edge of the plate to separate the overhanging pastry, and let the remaining dough sink into a perfect lining in the plate, ready for the filling. When the *tourtières* were done, she always made pinwheels with butter, brown sugar, and cinnamon with the extra pastry. *Pets de soeurs*, she called them, because they were "light sweet nothings".

He pictured the three of them fretting over the amount of broth each *tourtière* could safely withstand without surrendering the crispness of its crust. He remembered one Christmas when the entire holiday moved to the brink of disaster because his mother-in-law was so distressed at the soggy bottoms of her meat pies. And Laura, who had inadvertently doubled the amount of juices in each one, hadn't eased the situation by telling her mother that there were other things in life besides daughters having to keep the pot simmering. *Soigner la marmite*, she called it, with disdain. Yet she knew that the role her mother played in this yearly ritual was too crucial to be minimized or dismissed.

He looks forward to a quiet evening and hopes no

one will expect him to go to midnight mass this year. If he's to behave half-decently on Christmas day he'll have to turn in earlier than the ungodly hour when that merciless ceremony usually ends. In any event, no one ever really wants to go to midnight mass any more. Religion doesn't play an important role in his marriage, it never played a role at all except for the time his in-laws took it upon themselves to have David baptized when he was a baby. Laura acknowledged that she'd known about it but hadn't thought it important enough to turn it into an issue. Since it pleased her parents she would ignore it, and since she knew it would offend Geoffrey if he found out, she wouldn't tell him. A few Latin words and water sprinkled on a baby's forehead wouldn't leave any permanent damage, she said. She made light of it, paraphrasing from the Book of Judges: "Oh well, these days everyone does what's right in her own eyes." But Geoffrey hadn't been in a compromising mood. His views on religion weren't as erratic as his wife's, and the intrusion outraged him. This was his son and no one had the right to use him to perpetuate primitive rites and beliefs. If Laura didn't have solid ground on which to stand on religious issues, his was the *terra firma* from which reason prevailed. He made it clear that his in-laws were not to interfere with the raising of his children, especially when it came to religion. That was the end of it—although after Louise's birth his mother-in-law hinted in passing that in an emergency it was acceptable for a lay person to baptize a newborn baby, and he suspected she might have baptized Louise herself. Cradled her in her arms while giving her a bath and, tracing a cross on her forehead, whispered, "I baptize you in the Name of the Father, the Son, the Holy Ghost." The irony of his daughter secretly christened in the name of a father, but not him. His daughter bound to an old wives' tale, and undoubtedly Laura and her mother savoured the covertness of it all, the two of them thick as thieves.

The fact is, Laura's mother has always been too pragmatic to be a devout Catholic, but her pragmatism also cautions her to protect all her options. "They won't give us a proper burial if we don't go to mass once in a while," she says to justify an occasional attendance. As far as she's concerned the Church expects more than it gives, when it should be the other way around. She always feels vindicated when the Church gets caught, as she's very fond of saying, "with its own pants down". Last summer she relished telling everyone, especially her devout sisters, that she had just read two books about an American cardinal who hoarded so much money that he had to be protected by the Mafia. When she heard of the sexual and physical abuse of children by priests and brothers at several institutions across Canada she shrugged her shoulders in contempt. "Men don't control their urges any better when they're wearing a dress. Do you know what the actress said to the bishop, who was wearing a surplice and swinging his incense vessel?" she'll ask Louise and David. "Love your dress, darling, but your purse is on fire," and she'll laugh at her own irreverence. While she condemns these aberrations, she also perceives them as unfortunate examples of human frailty, a frailty that always seeks refuge in unlimited authority. Such phrases as "go forth and invade lands, slaughter men, women, sheep, and asses with the edge of a sword" were never meant to be taken literally. "You always have to see past the story," she'll add.

As for Laura, it's the choreography of gestures and words, the allegorical figures who people myths and liturgies, that still draw her to rituals. If part of her is relieved at not having to attend midnight mass, another part feels cheated at having to forgo the spectacular ceremony. Her ambivalence has nothing to do with creed or the coming of a messiah, but with the miraculous aura that surrounded the ritual when she was a child. Just as the possibility of miracles is the most cherished belief of a child, it is also the most cherished child of belief. As such, it is difficult to give up.

It always astonishes Geoffrey how easily Laura enters fictions, meanders in and out of stories her mother and father told her when she was a girl, aware that they belong to some other realm, a collective memory. Laura is the only person he knows who looks upon stories, the telling of them, as part of reality. Even if the stories aren't true, they represent the power of an imagination that is. It's the power of fiction that conceives messiahs, she said when she attempted to explain to him what Christmas still meant to her. Without that power there would be no Saviour or annunciatory angels, no oracles, no idle shepherds or wise men. As a child she imagined, or perhaps someone told her, that on Christmas night, at the exact stroke of midnight, animals would suddenly begin speaking human words at every crossroad of the world. And it was usually on Christmas night that the men in the lumber camps, where her father had been a waterboy when he was nine years-old, were seen riding the witch-canoes. He had told her, when she was a girl, about the enchanted boats skirting church steeples, as they carried the men through the skies, to their sweethearts or wives, when the roads into town were obstructed by snow. She knew, even then, that this was an improbable tale, but she believed it could happen, simply because her father, the only boy in a camp, had imagined he could see the canoes and that was as good as true.

What Laura misses most about midnight mass is that magic stroke of a universal clock when an entire congregation gathered under one roof and chanted in a language no one understood, though it was a common language. A story located somewhere beyond speech. *Kyrie Eleison, Christie Eleison,* she sang, off key, every year around Christmas, as if each year the song emerged from some mysterious depth and released a language she could make her own because it was not language; at least, not one she ordinarily spoke or understood. *Kyrie Eleison, Christie Eleison.* Familiar, alien, it released the limits of ordinary speech.

For Laura, the foreign tongue of prayer yearns for a target that is seldom God. It pleads for the restoration of something that's been lost. A language prior to language when the world was but a dream. A language prior to splitting when a voice in the darkness uttered, let there be light, and speech was deemed as morning's gift.

She misses the walk home after mass at three or four o'clock in the morning when, dead tired, she trailed behind her parents like an unwinding narrative, grateful it was almost time for everyone to open presents. Wet snow and the smell of incense clinging to her clothes, the moon caught in a network of winter branches, a benediction in which family, friends, strangers, and even nature collaborated. These images were once central to her life. How did they become too worn?

THE UNION

The year after we returned to Timmins from our two weeks on *mon oncle* Ti-Roc's farm, my father began working double shifts. Six days a week he diamond-drilled at the Hollinger mines from seven in the morning to three in the afternoon, and from four to midnight he tended bar at the Goldfield Hotel. After two years of saving every possible penny from the two jobs he bought a small hotel, the Union in Ansonville, a mile down the road from the pulp-and-paper town of Iroquois Falls. It faced the railway tracks and, beyond the tracks, Mike One-Arm's. I don't know how Mike lost his arm, someone said he'd sold it, but it was his house and he always had girls working for him.

When I first heard that Mike's was a cathouse I watched for cats. When they failed to materialize I looked up cathouse in my English dictionary and discovered a surprisingly long list of cat words: *catbird catcall catgut cat hook.* I was stunned to learn that *catholic* was defined as universal and broad in sympathies and interest. . . . *Catnap cat-o'-nine-tails cat's cradle cat's eye.* I liked cat's eye. The opalescent reflections from within. But my favourite was *catechu.* The residue from the heartwood of acacia.

acacia woody leguminous plants of warm regions
having pinnate leaves and bearing clusters of white
or yellow flowers that yield gum.

There was a *cat's foot,* a *cat's paw,* a *cattail,* a *catwalk,*
but I never did find a house for cats.

My bedroom window, which overlooked the parking
lot of the hotel, was a good vantage point from which to
observe the comings and goings of my dad's customers.
This was where men came out of the beverage room for a
breath of fresh air, or to take a leak, meet with someone
else's wife, or play with themselves. This was where they
decided to cross over to Mike's, especially on Saturday
nights, and where women screeched over men who picked
fights, and where couples made out leaning against two-
door Studebakers or in the back seats of four-door sedans.

Eventually all the town's people passed through that
parking lot. The beautiful blonde Polish woman with the
jealous husband who always screamed at her, "Once a
whore always a whore." They were found in their house
one Labour Day weekend, dead from a murder suicide.

whore from OE *hore* and L *carus* dear; n. 1. a
prostitute; 2. a woman who practises unlawful
sexual intercourse for hire. see *CHARITY.*

charity from OF *charité* and L *carus* dear and *caritas*
Christian love; n. 1. kindness or help for the
needy; 2. a gift for benevolent purposes; 3. lenient
judgement of others.

There was *Taraud,* who had a screw loose and delivered coal and picked up garbage and old clothes in a horse-
drawn cart.

There was Baby Elephant, the borderline case. Three
hundred pounds teetering on barely visible pumps as she

paraded down Main Street in elaborate flowered hats, with a retinue of six highly excitable chihuahuas:

Here comes Baby Elephant
Baby Baby Elephant
Her bum's so wide she can't wear pants
Her dance will send you in a trance

There was Le Noir, the tailor, the first man I was to see totally naked. I was passing his shop one afternoon and there he was standing in his picture window without a stitch on. The only feature I remember clearly is his one tooth at the side of his mouth when he grinned. At the time I interpreted his behaviour as rebellion against his profession, but that was before I heard he was a pervert.

pervert from F *pervers per* through or by means of *vers* a line of writing; or L *vertere* to turn; n. one who has turned to error, especially in religion; opposed to convert; v.t. to turn another way; to turn from truth; to divert from a right use; to lead astray; to misinterpret designedly.

There existed between Ansonville and Iroquois Falls an invisible but palpable line that divided the two towns. Although physically they were only separated by a road and a field, it was clear from the first week after we moved to Ansonville that the people from Iroquois Falls were not our kind of people, their town not our kind of town. The two were as different as night and day, as the English and the French.

Iroquois Falls was unlike most northern towns in that it hadn't sprouted from scattered shanties. When the Abitibi Pulp and Paper Company decided to build a mill there in the early twenties they hired industrial developers to design a model town to complex specifications. If executives, chemists, and engineers were willing to sacrifice city living for a hinterland, they deserved more than the bare necessities, so the houses were planned according to theories of high-priced architects. A nine-hole golf course and club house were built in the same expert fashion as exclusive city clubs, and Iroquois Falls was the only town for miles with two clay tennis courts.

"When your grandfather came home from doing carpentry work on the houses in Iroquois Falls when I was a little girl, he always had wondrous things to report," my mother told me when we moved near the model town. "I often went with him to see for myself. For a quarter you could preview roadshows of moving pictures with full symphony orchestras, before they opened on Broadway at two dollars a seat." My mother was only fourteen when she resolved to name her first daughter after a favourite actress.

There were many features in the houses of the new Abitibi town that those in Cochrane didn't have, and one that my mother noticed in particular were shelves. Shelves for books built on each side of a fireplace, some of them with glass doors, especially if the books were bound in leather. They were, my mother noticed, almost always English books.

From what I've been told there was little money for luxuries when my parents married, certainly none for shelves of books, but when I was three my mother purchased a series of Junior Classics, volumes of The Young Folks' Shelf published by Collier & Son of New York. Each volume was thematically classified, each classic story condensed and retold to make it more accessible to a child. She'd bought them from a door-to-door salesman who'd agreed she could pay for them on an instalment plan, a few dollars a month from the food money.

It was an extravagant acquisition that had to be kept from my father, so for a while the books remained hidden at the back of a clothes closet, stacked against a wall that enclosed the water pipes for the only sink in the house. By the time my mother discovered that the pipes leaked, most of the books had been sitting in water and all of them bore various degrees of water damage. This did not deter her from reading the books to me over and over again from the time I was four—which is probably why, as an adult, I have never been able to read Cervantes without a pervasive smell of mould.

The cover of each volume was a different colour, my favourite a purplish blue with only a small water stain at the right corner. *Heroes and Heroines.* The preface explained that this great treasure-house of stories was to the English race what the stories of Ulysses and Aeneas were to the Greeks and Latins. The high nobility, dauntless courage, and gentle humility of Arthur and his knights had, over centuries, left their own indelible mark in the shaping of the English character, since no one can help but imitate what he admires most.

After a few months in Ansonville, my parents decided that the Union Hotel was not the best environment for me. They were also concerned that after the separate school in Ansonville I would have to attend the only high school in the area, Iroquois Falls Secondary, which was exclusively English. As much as they wanted me to learn English, they also wanted me to maintain my French. In any case, my mother kept reminding me that the people of Iroquois Falls were not our kind of people.

We spent most of that first summer in Ansonville preparing me for Le Pensionnat Notre-Dame de Lourdes

in Sturgeon Falls and Les Filles de la Sagesse. My mother
sewed tags bearing number 199 on pairs of black stockings, two black dresses, underwear, everything I was
required to take with me, and I checkmarked the prospec-
tus as I placed each item in my brown metal trunk. She
would have welcomed the opportunity to go to a convent
herself when her mother died, she tried to reassure me, but
her younger sister had gone instead. I was lucky to be an
only child, sisters meant rivalry and jealousies. I remember my astonishment when she told me that as a girl she
would save pennies over several weeks and buy herself
small tins of salmon which she ate in hiding so she
wouldn't have to share them with her three sisters. I had
always imagined my mother to be as selfless as her own
mother, and the image of her savouring the flakes of pink
flesh and small white vertebrae behind a weathered shed
didn't fit the image I'd carried of her up to then.

"A hotel is not a place to bring up a child," my mother
must have repeated a hundred times that summer. She has
always made everything around her function as practically
as possible: the strict order of her house; the care with
which she prepares meals; the attention she paid to the
hotel ledgers when the dollars and cents had to correspond
to the exact number of beer bottles and cigarette packs sold
each night; the pride she takes in not letting anyone take
advantage of her or her husband. Determined that this
new venture wouldn't end in failure like *mon oncle* Ti-Roc's
farm, my parents worked ceaselessly to ensure the Union's
success, but because they were so busy the hotel also
became an unseemly place for a child. If, as with so many
mothers, my mother's energy often seems limitless and
unselfconscious, it is also often in conflict with her moth-
ering role. It's not always practical to have children

around.

There is also her fascination with the mechanism of precision. She's always the first to figure out what's wrong with a malfunctioning appliance and, when she can't fix it herself, always the first one to tell someone how it should be done. "We'd been given a clock as a wedding present and I wanted to understand how it worked so I took it apart one afternoon, and when your father came home he found me in tears because I couldn't get it to work again. Of course, that was due mainly to the quality of the clock," she adds, making sure I understand that the deficiency lay in the cheap gift, not in her mechanical abilities.

For reasons that must have suited their sense of humour, my parents were married on Halloween night. Trick or treat, my mother chuckles every anniversary. In the only snapshot of their wedding, my father is wearing a pale felt hat and spats, and my mother is in sepia fur. Simulated lamb, she explained to the seamstress when she had it cut and restyled into a coat, bonnet, and muff for me when I was five years old.

More and more I look like my mother, although as a child I was always told I resembled my father. So many daughters grow into their mothers, at least part of us does. The startling frown as I pass a window or a mirror. Perhaps that's why, when a detail doesn't fit the image I carry of her, I become both fascinated and afraid of the new dimension. Afraid the contradiction will turn her away from who I think she is. The perfect model of love.

I was as fascinated as I was apprehensive about going away to school. Excited by the new adventure but bewildered by a list of regulations that forbade so much. It was against the rules to bring books or any reading material and I would have to leave my volumes of The Young Folks'

Shelf at home. It was like parting with a major lifeline. These volumes were my only brothers and sisters.

The month before leaving I read some of the stories so many times that I practically knew them by heart— especially one of my favourites, "The Old Woman and the Knight", from *Heroes and Heroines*. I yearned for secrets as purposeful as those held by the old woman. She had powers similar to my mother's, powers that would see her through anything, anywhere. My mother would have known how to handle the knight, she would have known the answer to the riddle put before him by the Queen. I yearned for the nobility and courage of King Arthur's court, qualities that could have served me so well away from home. King Arthur's knights were as commanding as Catholic priests but they weren't as dour. When they did forget their knighthood pledges and overstep their boundaries they were always repentant and showed courage in the end. Even when the King made an example of an erring knight and sentenced him to die according to the strict letter of the law, as in my favourite story, the Queen intervened and gave the knight a second chance. And what a redemption it was!

"You are still in danger of losing your life," the Queen warned the knight, "but I will grant you freedom on the condition that you find me the answer to a particular question. To save your life you must tell me and my court what it is that women most desire. If you cannot now give me the answer you shall have a year and a day in which to learn it. Do your best and take great care, for if at the end of that period you still don't know, you will be found and put to death."

The knight could not guess the answer at once

so he pledged to return at the end of a year and a day, and he went away feeling great anguish. How was he to find the answer to such a difficult riddle? He wandered far, asking everyone he met what it was women loved best, but nowhere could he find two people who agreed. Some told him the answer was honour, others, riches or fine clothing, yet others insisted it was flattery and beauty that women loved above everything else. But none of these pleased the knight, for he knew in his heart they were not right.

One day, as he made his way through the forest, he saw a strange but wonderful sight. In a glade a ring of ladies were dancing, but as he drew nearer to see if by chance he might gain his answer, they all vanished. No one remained except for an old woman sitting on the grass, withered, poor, and ugly. "Sir knight," she said, "where are you going? This road leads no place. Tell me your errand and perchance I can help you. We old folk have knowledge of many things."

"Old mother," he said, "I am as good as dead if I cannot discover the answer to a riddle put to me by my Queen."

"What is this riddle?" the old woman asked with a glimmer in her dark eyes.

"I must find out the mystery of what it is that women love best. What is it a woman wants above all else? If you could help me, I would reward you well." And the knight told her the conditions on which his life was spared.

"Give me your word here and now that you will do the next thing I ask of you if it is in your power," said the hag, "and I will tell you the answer."

"I give my word," the knight replied, delighted with such an easy pact.

"Then your life is safe," she said, and whispered a word in his ear, and bade him to pluck up his courage, and together they rode to court.

Upon their arrival, the Queen and her company of ladies gathered to hear the young knight speak. "I have kept my word faithfully," he announced. "I am here on the day appointed, to answer the Queen's question. The answer she desired to what women want above all else is simple. It is power that women want most, power over their lives. If this is not the right answer, then do with me as you wish."

The Queen and the women agreed that the knight had saved his life by his reply. But when their verdict was made known, the old hag cried: "Give me justice, Lady Queen, before your court departs. I am the one who gave the knight the key to your riddle, and he in turn gave me his word that he would do what I ask if it is within his power. Now, before this court, I ask you, sir, to take me for your wife, and remember it was I who saved your life."

"Alas!" said the knight, astonished, "I did give my word, but will you not ask some other thing of me? Take all my riches if you wish but, I pray of you, let me go free."

"No," insisted the old woman. "Though I be old and poor and ugly I would not let you go for all the gold on earth. I will be your wife and love or you will perish. There is no other choice."

"My love!" he cried. "Nay, rather my death! Alas that any of my race should suffer such dishonour!" But all the knight's entreaties were of no avail. He had no choice but to keep his word and marry the old hag. And a mournful wedding he made of it. He took his new bride to his house, feeling not at all like a happy lover. On the contrary, her first words to him as they sat in the garden under the full moon intensified his sorrow.

"Dear husband, you have not uttered a word to me all evening. Is it the custom of the King's court for every knight to neglect his wife? I am your own true love who saved you from your death. I have not done you wrong, yet with your groans and your glum looks you act towards me like a madman who has lost his senses. Tell me what I have done amiss, and I will set it right."

"You cannot set it right," said the knight, his voice laden with grief. "Do you wonder that I am ashamed to have married one of such mean birth, so poor and old and ugly?"

"That is the cause of your self-pity?" the old woman asked.

"How could it be otherwise?" the knight replied.

"That is unfortunate, dear sir, for I have the power to set it right," countered the wife, "but you speak too proudly of your high birth and expectations. Such pride is worth nothing. A noble nature is not made only by high birth or wealth. You say I am low-born, old, and ugly. Well, choose which you would desire me to be—as I am: poor, old, and ugly but a true and faithful wife; or young, rich, but fickle, fond of vain pleasures, always emptying your purse and wounding your faithful love."

The knight had always longed for a wife who was beautiful, rich, and young, but he was moved to shame by his wife's words. "My lady, my dear wife, I put myself into your hands. Choose that which will honour you. What you wish is enough for me."

"Then you grant me power to choose as I please!" she exclaimed.

"Yes, dear wife," he answered, "this is how it should be."

"Kiss me," said the wife, "and let us quarrel no more. I will be both to you—fair and true. I will be as good a wife as ever there was one, if we both share this power."

Resigned, the knight looked up to kiss his wife, but instead of the withered old woman he expected, his eyes fell upon the fairest woman he had ever seen.

THE PROPHET OF THE RAND

From the time he was a boy my father was aware that people were coming from all over the world to find work in Northern Ontario. Those were exciting times, speculation running like liquid gold throughout the country and beyond. Some called it "moon fever", others called it "gold fever", and the ailment had no quick remedy. In spite of men disappearing in blizzards, trails as impervious as old maids, snow blindness and the slow madness that creeps over men when they've been "bushed" for too long, thousands of people made their way north each year: high-school drop-outs from Toronto or Calgary, clad in thin overalls and pointed city shoes; middle-aged men who had hardly survived the Depression; engineers in tweeds, looking more like fox-hunting squires than mining prospectors; the "DPs", who spoke just enough English to understand the superlatives of the thousands of prospectuses that had reached them overseas. All were ready to risk the little they had for the chance of striking it rich.

My father met many of these men when he worked at the Hollinger. Most of them had given up prospecting by then and gone underground, their faces marked by the grey sameness that comes from working gloomy mine shafts. He'd come across many of these men, or men like them, when he'd worked in the lumber camps. Their hopes had been high then, their faces reflecting their aspirations, their names a hodgepodge of different backgrounds: MacDonald, O'Rourke, Hawkins, Bélanger, Manzini, Ostojich, Shulak, Landowaki, Schneider, Holgevac. There was one notorious foreigner known as the Prophet of the Rand, because some people are better remembered by how they endure than by their real names. The Prophet had made a career of tracking gold in all its forms. The one ray of light in the darkness, he often said.

A visitor to the gold camps of the twenties and thirties would have been astounded at how brisk business was. The men could always be divided into two groups: those who were about to take the trails and those who had just returned. The former, cleanshaven, equipment patently fresh from the store, kept busy sorting out dog-harnesses, packing chuck-bags, and studying maps, while the latter, wild-haired and bearded, sprawled about smoking, relating tales of frostbite and starvation. This was how the Prophet came to be famous throughout the north. In the light of a few lanterns framed in thick smoke, men in mackinaws and moccasins leaned against the backpacks and snowshoes that festooned the walls and bunkbeds and listened to him. His scouting for gold around the world had provided him with enough material to keep the men entertained for months. Or perhaps it was the other way around—his flair for storytelling may well have been the catalyst for his explorations. He could discuss anything from Shakespeare to skinning a wildcat. In an accent none of the men had heard before, and in images none of them had ever imagined, he spoke of lines of ox-carts trailing over a ridge that rose six thousand feet above a foreign sea.

He could imitate the sound of its waters at different times of the year, and for the first time in their lives men who were more familiar with the sounds of wolves and tethered huskies and the crunching of snow under their feet heard stampedes of ostriches across dry fields, the barking of baboons in ravines, the deep-voiced droning of kaffirs at sunset. "No matter where you travel, these remain in the eye and the ear," the Prophet told them. For the first time, they saw images and heard sounds so different from what they knew that it was as if their world had been turned upside down.

But the Prophet's best stories were about men, particularly men who spent their lives devising ways of speeding up their wheel of fortune. In an accent so distinctive that the men never thought of questioning its credibility, he would tell them of fly-by-night prospectors who could talk anyone out of a month's salary with promises of fail-proof stocks. The pet names he gave to schemes gone awry became codes for the camp's inside jokes. "Want to invest in Sunken Sucker?" someone would ask a greenhorn, shaking his head and spitting tobacco juice from the corner of his mouth. "Or what about Golden Shaft, want to buy some Golden Shaft?" they snickered, although they all agreed that Golden Shaft had been different, it had been run right, nobody was to blame because the funds had run out before anyone could tell if there was gold there. No, they didn't mind taking risks if the cards ran fair, and when they didn't, they made the best of it. If in a few weeks everyone, even the "DPs", had mastered the camp's lingo and knew what it meant to be taken for a ride or to the cleaners, lose their shirt, get their leg pulled, everyone also knew how to get on with it, resigned to the fact that their month's salary was probably being spent on a couple of sweeties up there in Toronto. You couldn't live so close to gold and not be an optimist.

One of the men's favourite pastimes was guessing where a new man came from by his accent. The Prophet, who had travelled the world over, could detect the most subtle nuance of a person's speech and identify anyone's country. When he'd lived in that damned country he used to call home, he'd been able to identify the country of origin of any white South African, no matter how many generations it was since the family had immigrated. He'd even been able to tell what tribal group a black South African came from by the way he spoke Afrikaans, whether he was a Zulu or a Xhosa, and he would pronounce the latter with a clicking vibration in his throat, as if a cricket had suddenly unfolded from a tremor of warm sand. But as far as his own accent was concerned, it no longer belonged to a mother country. Oh yes, he'd once been from around the Great Rand Reefs, but his ties and roots had been washed away like the tilted bed of that magnificent seashore. That was where his heart was, in the waters that surrounded the ridge of a gold-bearing sea, and his alliance remained with the small skeletons that formed the foundations of its barriers. The Prophet always spoke like this, holding the key to many of the men's dreams. He explained how the reefs of South Africa had been as mottled, with gold, as the varicosed legs of a woman who'd born twenty children. But Northern Ontario had as many of these "auriferous rocks", he'd add, the r's rotating in his mouth as the men envisioned giant veins of gold running along the massive leg of a reef. But that was the past, the Prophet insisted, and here was the future. In Canadian gold.

According to the Prophet, he only worked for the

best or the biggest. South Africa had been unchallenged as the largest gold producer of the world for a long time but now it was threatened by a Canadian mine, the Hollinger. Barely a few years old, it was setting up new production records one day and tearing them down the next. More than ten thousand tons of ore were hoisted up its central shaft daily, enough to fill 150 freight cars. Three thousand men and ten million dollars' worth of machinery pushed to their limit couldn't strip a mine in a person's lifetime. And that was only one mine; there was talk of enough gold for a dozen more. Men could burrow into the earth for half a mile for fifty years and not run out of gold. It was even possible that it was beyond human reach. "Ah yes," the Prophet would say, "that's where the future is, somewhere beyond reach." It was a challenge he couldn't resist.

Before leaving South Africa, the Prophet had wanted to see his continent one last time. He told the men that he'd travelled its width and length, searching for new discoveries, but there was nothing there that hadn't existed for someone else before him. Victoria Falls, the highest falls in the world, had been discovered by some bloke named Livingstone; Lake Tanganyika, the world's longest and deepest fresh-water lake, had been claimed by a John Speke and a Sir Richard Burton. Why, he wondered, had these magnificent bodies of water not been located before the bloody English got there? Had they been such an intrinsic part of the local people's life, like the trees and the weather, that they had failed to notice them until a foreigner came along and gave them new names? Could the people have taken them so much for granted that they'd simply been misplaced, waiting to be rediscovered by someone coming upon them for the first time? Was it the bloody English who had discovered the sad cooing of

South Africa's favourite bird, the Prophet would ask, cupping his mouth with his hands to duplicate the heavy sigh of a bush dove.

After ten or twelve hours of prospecting in sub-freezing temperatures, the men would gather around the Prophet and listen to him relate how he had travelled across a continent charged with the constant buzzing of a glaring sun. A few months before leaving Africa, he'd heard that farther north, in the hinterland of the Sierra Leone, there existed an orchid the colour of gold, unseen anywhere else. He had even imagined, although he knew this was impossible, that there existed a method, an alchemical process, of extracting gold that wasn't limited to mud and rock. What if gold could be obtained from the living flesh of a flower?

For several months the Prophet became an orchid stalker. Orchids were being shipped to the colonies and orchid hunting was becoming big business. It was dangerous work; one man named Schroeder disappeared and was never heard of again. But the Prophet, buoyed by the hope of a rare orchid named after him, infiltrated forests, braved natives, torrential rains, rapids, floods, poisonous snakes, until one day he fell upon the leathery arching lips of a small orchid the most brilliant gold he had ever seen. Its mobile lip, barely tipped in dull red, was the most perfect of flowers. For weeks he continued to track the species down. As soon as one orchid wilted he searched for another, until finally fever drove him away from the Sierra Leone towards a more durable species of gold.

To support his prospecting in Ontario, the Prophet often worked a few months at a time at the Hollinger, although it was reported that the last time he'd worked there he'd left under questionable circumstances. He was often seen ranging the woods and lakes of Northern Ontario for discoveries that promised to be even bigger and better than the Hollinger. "It's comin', this country's coming, it's only so long now, just more or less," he'd say, his eyes drifting past the men as if onto a screen. "I can see this country opening up, the greatest mining belt in all the world. There'll be mineshafts all the way from Rouyn to Northern Manitoba, and they will make millionaires galore."

Eventually the Prophet disappeared from Northern Ontario, although his name came up now and then and apparently he'd been seen somewhere in the North-West Territories. Gossip was spreading about him, not all of it complimentary. One person claimed that he'd known him in South Africa and that the Prophet had been caught once too often smuggling gold out of the mines and no one would hire him down there any more. Someone else confirmed that the same thing had happened at the Hollinger.

My father was working part-time tending bar at the Goldfield Hotel when a couple of guys who'd just flown in from "nowhere", one of those places you couldn't locate on a map yet, came into the bar one night. As Willie Wylie and Pete Racine explained, their job was to scout the Far North's newest camps, examine new claims, and see what a rush was all about. Everyone was abuzz with a recent discovery at the Eldorado gold mine but this time the excitement wasn't about gold. One of the most precious elements available had been found near Gordon Lake. Radium. An element so rare it was running at $500,000 an ounce, and it was believed that the Great Bear Lake area, extending all the way to Gordon Lake, held one of the most important caches in the world. A guy by the name of Gilbert LaBine had found radium ore at Great Bear Lake in the early thirties and set the first rush in motion, but then came these spectacular discoveries so far north you could only go in by plane.

As Willie Wylie and Pete Racine told it, going that far north was a spectacular trip. They took off from Cameron Bay, skimmed the point of the cape on a ski and a wing, crossed the bluff escarpment of the Conjuror Mountains, and cut south across the frozen expanse of Hottah Lake. There the pilot would abandon his map, place the sun in relationship to his southeasterly course, and swing off across 250 miles of uncharted terrain. The plane, weighed down by sled dogs, carriole sleighs, snowshoes, rifles, dynamite, cases of canned goods, droned for two hours over snow-covered lakes and stumps of dun-brown timber. After an hour or so the pilot would point down to a river, bring out his map, and run his finger in a line from the northeast to the southwest. They had re-entered the geographer's domain, and the pilot, spotting a long, sinuous body of water, would tilt the plane's nose like a divining rod and begin its downward glide.

It was in Gordon Lake that Willie and Pete had run into an eccentric chap known as the Prophet. He'd heard of a substance that glowed like the moon when used on clocks, so that it was always possible to tell what time it was even in the dark. "The Prophet said radium was not a stable element," they would relate, trying to keep a straight face, tapping their index fingers to the sides of their heads, indicating that perhaps the Prophet was none too stable himself.

The Prophet knew of a couple in France, the Curies, who had predicted that an element they had discovered while working with uranium would be the turning point of modern physics. Radium. It had to do with atoms and energy, and the Prophet wanted in on it because he said that was where the future was.

"The Prophet hadn't realized," Willie and Pete continued, practically laughing themselves off their chairs, "that you can't just stuff radium up your arse the way he used to smuggle gold out of the Hollinger. People said he used to cram in so many gold nuggets he could hardly stagger out of there. A real con man who was so good at telling a story it took people months or years to wise up to him. When the poor bastard learned that tons of ore were required to extract just one ounce of radium, he was one sorry fellow. "'Yes it's coming,'" Willie and Pete would say, mocking the Prophet's accent, "'this country is coming, it's only so long now, more or less.'"

It was the Prophet, however, who had the last laugh. He left Canada a disillusioned albeit very wealthy man. Wherever he was heading next, he must have taken with him a fresh collection of stories, tales about mineral belts extending thousands of miles, all the way from Quebec to just east of Hudson Bay. He must have told of a town called Yellowknife where there was so much gold you could cut through it like butter. He must have told about the polar bears the men had to face to get to the radium up there in the North-West Territories. He would undoubtedly relay how he had been fortunate enough to experience the most remarkable discoveries in the most romantic settings of the world. The biggest and the best. Here he would no doubt pause for effect. "The biggest and the best," he'd emphasize, "before so many of the woods were destroyed and the lakes scummed. Before the game was scattered and the refuse of the modern mining colossus was strewn all about the countryside. As a matter of fact, there's little splendour left in that damn country I used to call home," he'd have told his listeners, in his newly acquired Canadian accent. "Those people up there are so busy extracting all the gold from their ground, there'll soon be nothing left. Those people in Northern Canada just don't seem to understand that even the most rugged landscapes are as perishable, as fleeting, as orchids from the Sierra Leone."

CONFESSION

...the vision of an infinite flesh is a madman's vision...

Clarice Lispector

Now that she's been accelerated to a higher grade, math means algebra and geometry, but Soeur Lucienne says it isn't much use to girls. Plane geometry, Soeur explains, is good for boys when they want to figure out dimensions like the flat surface of baseball fields, and she draws points, lines, and planes of a baseball diamond on the blackboard. It's useful to astronomers to roam the altitudes of stars and planets, and draftsmen, by reducing three-dimensional space to two dimensions, can sketch maps of different countries and travel anywhere they please. Soeur Lucienne says it was probably because of his keen sense of geometry that Columbus assumed the earth was round before he set out to plough the seas.

For a child who still believes in miracles, the strict rules of algebra or geometry leave little room for the miraculous, yet there is a commanding quality to the exact. If A equals B equals C. The unnamed, disguised as letters, marching towards a resolution that is unchanging, each symbol a passkey to the unknown.

If A equals B equals C. The authority of the perfect triangle, like the Trinity. It knows everything, sees everything, gapes from above the door of study hall and scrutinizes the bowed skulls it's about to penetrate. It invades playgrounds, bathrooms, refectories, prowls dormitories, follows the small hand brushing against soft genitals or budding breasts under bedsheets. Obsessive, lugubrious, it pervades even dreams in its insatiable thirst for young girls' aberrations, its bloated eye a background for the forbidden image it yearns to receive. If A equals B equals C. Mute symbols that range each and every thing in its proper place. The equals and the unequals.

When her parents decided to send her to a *pensionnat* it was in the name of a classical education, and there's little doubt they believed that. Everything that hurt was for her own good.

For the first three months she could barely utter a word. Whenever anyone spoke to her, asked her name, her voice drowned in the frantic beating of a heart about to unfold in her chest, the fluttering of an injured bird. A heart as raw and mangled as the life-size Sacred Heart at the end of the corridor.

Year after year the Sacred Heart welcomed the new girls with open arms and bleeding hands, and in spite of its bland expression it looked sinister. Once the forbidding doors opened, exposing a labyrinth of corridors, the parents delivered their daughters to creatures wearing bird-in-flight coiffes and ominous crucifixes tucked inside their aprons. The statue at the end of the corridor conveyed only one message. Hope for nothing and there will be nothing to fear.

But convent life never raises itself above fear. Detection and punishment hover in every act or thought, everything is steeped in dread. This is the means by which convent girls advance towards an order different from other children, the anxiety of being abandoned by their families replaced by the worst fear of all: the fear of sin. The endless rites of penance. Atonement, purification.

There will be confession once a week, Mère Supérieure whispered to the new girl as she showed her the chapel on the first day, genuflecting before a smaller Sacred Heart. Dipped the girl's fingers into the holy water, guiding her hand to her forehead, *au nom du Père*, her chest, *du Fils*, her shoulders, *et du Saint-Esprit*, and led her towards the sentinel box in the corner.

After the constraints of one week's silence, at confession she is encouraged to speak as much as she pleases. *Dis-moi tes péchés mon enfant.* Within the suffocating confinement of the confessional she is compelled to murmur, into an ear behind the grille, the unworthiness of her errors. The foreboding Eye from study hall has been replaced by the foreboding Ear. How long since your last confession. Have you had unkind thoughts. Have you had impure thoughts. Did you touch yourself there. Did you let anyone touch you there. Why were you alone with Christine in the dormitory. Why did you pull the coiffe off Soeur Lucienne's head?

Anger, envy, greed, pride, laziness, disobedience, are all serious enough vices, to which the young girl willingly admits even if she doesn't always know what they mean. For the most part these are venial transgressions that merit only a few Pater Nosters or Ave Marias. Gluttony is almost never referred to; Père is well acquainted with the nuns' culinary skills.

It is another kind of sin that consumes the priest's mind. It is sins of the flesh that rob the confessional of its air, mortal sins, deadly sins. The flesh, *la chair*, the hush sound of its *shhh* seals it with disgrace, reduces the voices on each side of the grille to barely audible murmurs.

Flesh, the soft part of a mother's body, *shhh*. Bloody flesh, mucous flesh, entrails, organs, *shhh*. Nakedness, buttocks, penis, vagina, menstruation, *shhh*. Sex, *shhh*. The most doubtful parts of human nature, *shhh*. For these are the deadly sins that stain the soul, deface it until it caves in under the weight of its own decay, under the weight of its own flesh.

Only the voice on the other side of the grille can cleanse it. Only the wizardry of words, the fictive act of ablution, can redeem the soul from its eternal fate. *Que la passion de notre Seigneur Jésus-Christ, les mérites de la bienheureuse Vierge Marie, et de tous les saints, et tout ce que vous ferez de bien, supporterez de pénible, contribuent au pardon de vos péchés. Amen.* God's first language used to be Latin, but now it's French.

Since it's practically impossible, because of the unrelenting supervision, to commit most of the sins suggested to her, it isn't long before the young girl comes to understand that, for the most part, confession is a re-enactment of Père's vivid imagination. It's true, sometimes she does scandalous things like pulling the coiffe off Soeur Lucienne's head, but this is meaningless compared to touching oneself or someone else there. In any case, pulling the coiffe off Soeur's head is only Soeur's side of the story, and at confession only that side will be heard. There isn't much point explaining to Père that she was in the dormitory with Christine because everyone else had gone home for Thanksgiving and they were only reading a book that Madame Wickersham had lent them for the weekend. *Wuthering Heights*. They were enthralled with visions of crinolines and rituals of English tea and were doing nothing more than giggling over the mysterious Heathcliff, as dark and brutal a man as a young girl could imagine. They yearned to be his ministering angel, the beauty to his beast. "Be with me always, take any form, drive me mad," they were exclaiming when Soeur charged into the dormitory, asking why they were lurking there by themselves, sneaking *Dieu sait quoi* behind her back.

"Did you write the essay Mère asked you to write on *noblesse oblige?*"

"*Oui, mon Père.*" She had to write the essay after Soeur Lucienne reported her to Mère, but she still doesn't understand the correlation between reading a novel by an Englishwoman and the honourable behaviour expected from those of noble rank and birth. Those qualities have nothing to do with her. The Brontës and their Catherine held all the privileges, and *Wuthering Heights* was paradise.

It isn't long before the young girl realizes there's no point in explaining any of this in confession, just as she comes to accept the priest's skilful prodding. It isn't long before she comes to accept that what Père really wants to hear is her latent vileness, brought to light through her words, her speech. So when she feels her venial sins don't lend her confession enough weight, she invents bigger and better ones. Yes, someone touched me there. Who. Soeur Lucienne. Yes, after that I had bad dreams. Tell me your dreams.

IN THE LAND OF THE CHIMERAS

Ce ne sont que des chimères, Soeur Bernard mutters each night as she awakens the young girl from another dream. The wailing and moaning disturb the other girls and Soeur Bernard's cell is closest to the young girl's bed so she has inherited the troublesome task of waking her. *Ces rêves ne sont que des chimères.*

> **Chimère** *n.f. (*lat. chimaera, *chèvre). Monstre fabuleux, dont le corps tenait moitié du lion, moitié de la chèvre, et qui avait la queue d'un dragon. \\ Idée fausse, vaine imagination. Esprit chimérique \\Sans fondement; illusoire, utopique.*

Does the beast exist in English as well?

> **Chimera** from L chimaera goat. n. A she-monster in Greek mythology, usually with a lion's head vomiting flames. An imaginary monster; an illusion or fabrication of the mind; an unrealizable dream.

Chimeras do exist in both languages, everything does. Or perhaps in the Land of the Chimeras there is no difference between languages. The she-monsters of her sleep never speak as they scale the cloistering walls and invade the pale shadows of her dreams, the spaces left empty when she tries to appease the memories of home.

The sound of her dreams always comes to her in her mother's voice. She never sees her mother's face nor does the voice speak words, but the blanket of sound that wraps her, curls inside her, is the familiar voice of her mother, a sonorous whoosh like a heartbeat. Body talk.

This is the beginning of the dream. The sound of her mother's voice as they stand in front of a doorway which the young girl is expected to enter but which she resists. The wailing begins when she realizes that the mother wants her to proceed to the other side of the door without her, when she's expected to leave her mother on one side of the door and enter the land of the she-monsters.

It is said that in the Land of the Chimeras, young girls are kept in boxes to prevent them from growing; their lips are slit to prevent them from speaking, their skulls compressed to keep them from thinking. The results are so exotic that the she-monsters are often used for exhibition and profit, although these are not their only functions. When things go wrong in The Land of the Chimeras, the she-monsters usually shoulder the blame. In the Land of the Chimeras, the she-monsters are often sacrificed, a fate they willingly accept. For no matter how much their skulls have been compressed, their loneliness affords them a fuller understanding of these matters.

Like a dog that licks the hand of the person who beats it because it cannot escape its fate, the she-monster tries to soothe her assailants by drawing nearer to them. She even proclaims to love them, knowing there is no escaping the peculiar cruelties that turned her into her judges' scapegoat.

From the first week at the *pensionnat* the young girl

is unable to escape this dream, its vividness unaltered by interpretation or meaning. A child seldom wakes up to reassure herself that a nightmare is but a dream. She knows she is being carried to some other realm where landscapes are even more sinister than the icons and statues surrounding her during the day.

The sequence is always the same. Her mother's voice, the chimeras, the wailing, the waking into the darkness of the dormitory, followed by a peculiar feeling that haunts her for days. From the moment she arrived at the convent it has dogged her. An uneasy feeling that separates her from everyone else, and says, I'm myself and no one else and how did that come to be, how come I'm me? During those moments her sense of self is so powerful and lonely that if she were to die at that very instant it wouldn't matter, because she has already experienced all that can be experienced. There is within her a storehouse of everything she knows, everything she's learned and experienced, and all that is to come is only going to be a repeat of that knowledge. This is what the future is, then. Even if the events change, the feelings, the sadness, will remain the same. The future only holds more of the same. As such it has already been invented.

Later she will come to recognize that to be unlike everyone else is to be the same as all the others, each person being worth any other. Later she will come to understand that a nine-year-old's experience only seems repetitious and irrelevant, as if at nine she understood so much but now understands so little, as if an unravelling has taken place. As if she were moving towards a space where nothing exists.

Hope for nothing and there will be nothing to fear.

BABY BOA

If my father had written his stories instead of telling them he would have been a ribald writer. The year someone gave him illicit copies of Henry Miller's novels, my mother and I heard endless guffaws coming from behind the bathroom door every time he had a free moment. Even the photograph of Miller on one of the dust jackets must have produced a sense of kinship, the two of them looked so much alike; both fair, balding, wearing dark-rimmed glasses, my father's Norman features similar to Miller's Germanic face. But it was Miller the maverick and rebel that my father admired; the swagger, the pranks, the locker-room humour. My father has always felt more at ease in a world of men. Friends from fifty years ago are friends to this day, an old-age street gang with whom he can instantly share assumptions and responses.

"Henry Miller," my father would say as he came out of the bathroom, "is not above ordinary people. He knows about hockey, goes to dances, wrestling and boxing matches." As an amateur boxer he particularly appreciated this last detail. It proved that Miller's world was couched not in the esoteric but in the sweat and violence of young men who spent much of their time on the street. Everything else was false and derived. Above all, it was Miller's sense of irreverence that he admired. His contempt for society and its constraints, prudery, religious zeal. "*Les pisseuses*," my father always called the nuns on our way to the *pensionnat*, as if to remind me that even they were not above mockery, as if, by making them the target of his ridicule, he could displace with one epithet their authority and my misgivings.

Sex has always been a target of my father's humour, although, unlike Miller, his stories about women are relatively tame. Nor does he spare religious themes, his views on morality being as uncomplicated as his story plots or his *patois*. I've heard some of the stories at least a dozen times but I don't mind since each rendition grows new features, new configurations. Like Baby Boa and the circus. That story captures perfectly how my father saw himself as a young man and how he still wants to be seen. The face he likes to present to the world is that of a joker, a clown with a smiling mouth painted over a real mouth that usually points down, especially now that he's old.

The circus was coming to Timmins for a week, and the preacher, Billy Sunday, was hopping mad. The Ringling Brothers were not only exploiting unfortunate freaks of nature by exposing them to the public, but were using them as a front for the dissemination of sedition and perdition. At least, that's what Billy Sunday was declaring from his own portable tent.

Of course, to most French Canadians Billy Sunday was as good a sideshow as any. Everyone was familiar with him, especially during Prohibition, when he filled arenas across the country and came riding north on a trail of glory. He could draw the biggest names, from prominent clergymen to members of the Ontario government and, of course, their attending wives. Many of the women involved in the Temperance League held onto Billy's every word, each word delivered with more fury than the one before. He was a master. No one had ever heard preaching like this before, not even from a Catholic pulpit. Billy's elocution poured like Niagara discharging into the abyss: he raved, he roared, he paced the platform from end to end and for additional drama looked down into the crowd as into hell, and ordered the Devil to withdraw because the people in this northern part of the country were going all the way with God.

In spite of mannerisms that would have offended most people, Billy could carry an audience like nobody else. Even those who came to make fun of him were occasionally seduced by his equations of drink and vice, sobriety and happiness. This was a puzzle to many, because the only people they ever saw happy were the ones who'd had a few drinks. But it all figured. Billy Sunday was English and Prohibition was just another affliction invented by the English, a perverse lot whose obsession with alcohol was just some smokescreen. It was common knowledge that almost everyone made home-brew or mash and almost everyone was ready to pay for a recipe that would improve the quality and quantity of the product.

One guy my father knew made a good living following the circus from town to town carrying a large box of sealed envelopes. He would study the circus crowd, approach potential customers flushed by the promise of magic, and whisper that not only did he hold the secret of the world's best substitute for their favourite brands, but he was prepared to part with it for a scant twenty-five cents. As envelope and money changed hands he whispered to his clients that they should read the contents only in the safety of their homes:

> Chase a bullfrog for three miles and gather the hops. To the hops add 3 gallons of tan bark, 3 pints of shellac, and 6 bars of homemade soap. Boil the mixture for 36 hours and strain it through a W.W.I banner to keep it from working. Add one grass-hopper to give it a kick.

Perhaps that's why Billy Sunday didn't like the competition. The circus incited extravagant moods. His gatherings in Toronto had netted him over nine thousand dollars each and Billy estimated it was possible to make more if he could only get rid of homemade stills and intercept what was seeping into Ontario from the United States and Quebec. An immoral province where God had been unable to gain any ground where drink and other vices were concerned. The correlation between the consumption of liquor and the large families with which French Canadians saddled themselves was no mystery.

But praise the Lord, at least the railway police were trustworthy, and Christian. Just last week a shipment of fish, some sixty cases of sea fish, had left Quebec for a Western Ontario city, and there could be no doubt about it being genuine because the fish tails stuck out from the ends of nearly every crate. But praise the Lord, the camouflage hadn't deceived one conscientious and astute official; when he tweaked the fish tails sticking out, each and every one came away in his hand, bearing the unmistakable evidence of having been severed from the rest of the body by a sharp instrument. Naturally a search followed, and some sixty cases of Scotch were seized by the Ontario Government. It was worth going to Billy Sunday's meetings just to hear the stories.

Everyone had a story about Prohibition long after it was over; there's nothing like interdiction to stir the imagination. No one doubted, for example, that at one point there had been a sudden influx of dead bodies arriving in crude caskets from Quebec. A husband or sister or daughter working in the French province had died and was being shipped home for burial in Ontario, where the closest relatives lived. At first no one thought of opening the boxes to face decomposing corpses, but after a while it must have occurred to another conscientious and loyal railway official that there were a lot of Ontarians dying in Quebec. Furthermore, persons supposedly dead were materializing out of nowhere, so an investigation was launched. It soon became clear what the caskets had really contained.

You can't keep liquor from those who want it. Even in the most isolated bush areas the work gangs managed to get all the whisky they wanted and more. The breath of some guys at ten in the morning was enough to clear the air of black flies. The Inland Revenue was called in once to solve the mystery of the drunken lumberjacks, and what they found was nothing short of an engineering miracle: three stills travelling from site to site by canoe. The liquor wasn't just being sold from the canoes, it was being made right on them. Of course, you could also get contraband alcohol from St. Pierre and Miquelon. *Du whisky blanc. Si j'avais un peu d'argent, j'me bâtirais un restaurant. D'la bière par en arrière, du whisky blanc par en avant.*

The summer my father was seventeen, he worked for a man who made moonshine for blind pigs. That's when he started dreaming of owning his own bar. There existed a bond among young men who worked in blind pigs, a sense of mission and dedication against senseless laws. They'd get raided every once in a while, but the raids were mostly to provide the police with cheap liquor or have it tested for the lye some moonshiners added for an extra jolt. Some people had died from drinking too much lye-laden liquor. But the operation my father worked for was so clean he sold small flasks to pharmacies for medicinal purposes.

Even after Prohibition, people continued to make their own liquor because it was cheaper than buying it. *D'la poutine*, French Canadians called it, bran and sugar fermented in barrels near the stove, but the English called it mash. Some people used pressure cookers or stills but my father used *un alambic*, a contraption for refining and separating during distillation. After Prohibition the 4.4 per cent alcohol content of beer wasn't potent enough for some of the oldtimers so they added a little moonshine to it.

The first summer after my father left the lumber camp, there was a lot of commotion because both Billy Sunday and the circus would be in town at the same time. Although Prohibition had ended, Billy was still travelling, spreading the Word, and people were wagering as to who could draw the biggest crowd on Saturday, the last night of the circus. As far as my father was concerned it was no contest. The circus was very exciting in those days; the smell of dirty canvas and wood shavings, the animals, the warmed-over hot dogs, floss and popcorn, but mostly the people. Every night that week, my father and his friends, each equipped with a twelve-ounce flask, went to the circus and stayed until it closed, because Ronnie, one of my father's friends, had fallen for one of the Wonders of the World. A real wonder, too, but not in the same way as

Tom Thumb II and his wife, or the Frog Lady, whose skin was a peculiar shade of green and who could make her jowls and throat swell as big as a frog's when the caller fed her flies.

This was another kind of wonder. The woman Ronnie fell for didn't have anything freakish about her unless you thought sex was freakish. She was a seductress—the Snake Enchantress, they called her—whose real name was Carmelita. The first time they saw her she was standing on the outside platform with a boa constrictor draped around her shoulders and a rock python coiled around one of her thighs. She seemed indifferent to the calliope wheezing carnival music, and the raspy-voiced caller giving a flamboyant inventory of the delights waiting inside the large tent.

There was, my father conceded, something about Carmelita that was intriguing. There were no women like her up north. She was everything a man imagined a woman to be. Her tight-fitting skirt was gathered to one side of her hips below her bare midriff, a small hammock of satin and spangles cradled her breasts, and she wore open-toed snakeskin pumps with spike heels. Her eyebrows were like miniature crows painted in sharp angles above eyes that flashed as they scanned the crowd, and her wide mouth was a bright slash of carmine against white teeth.

"Step right up ladies and gentlemen and see the world's foremost reptile subjugator. What you see coiled around this pretty maiden's neck and shoulders is only a baby boa but on the inside platform you can view its mother if you step right up and purchase your tickets ladies and gentlemen. The mother of this baby is twenty-three feet long and weighs one hundred and twenty-five pounds, more than the little enchantress herself.

"Is it deadly? Yes. Why? Because it kills its prey with the constrictive power of its muscular coils. Ladies and gentlemen, it can sque-e-e-e-e-ze this daring young woman to death in fifteen seconds. Is the Enchantress frightened? Of course she is, ladies and gentlemen, wouldn't you be? But if you purchase your tickets and follow her inside you will witness how, with one word, she can command the snakes in her menagerie to leave their bed. You will see these vicious reptiles twist and curl towards their mistress and entwine her luscious body until she becomes a hissing monument of reptilian flesh. Step right up ladies and gentlemen and buy your tickets to the inner tent." As the Enchantress's eyes scrutinized the crowd with the go-to-hell look of the seasoned showgirl, they lit on Ronnie until their eyes locked. She then disappeared into the tent, which promised the World's Most Exotic and Curious People.

Inside, the tent was so hushed it was like entering a canvas cloister. Before getting to the snake box, the spectators were summoned by the Frog Lady, Tom Thumb II and his wife, and Mossa Singhalee the Fireproof Wonder from Ceylon. Mossa wielded a blowtorch across his bare chest and his eyeballs, applied a cherry-red iron to his tongue, and walked on white hot bars, but Ronnie wanted to get to the snake box.

It sat on the stage, about the size of a maiden's hope chest, its mirror-lined lid propped open so the snakes could be seen from ground level. They appeared larger than life, as anything does when reflected in a mirror, their colours intense, their markings boldly defined. One of them, the mother boa, was dark brown and black with saddles of tan along its back and a crimson red tail.

Another, a rock python, looked like an Oriental rug in striking patterns of pale browns and yellows. Later, after my father and his friends got to know Carmelita, she admitted that the snakes were totally harmless. She treated them like pets, each one slithering towards her when she called it by name.

Her favourite was Sully, the baby boa she carried around her neck when she was on the outside stage. She'd named it after a Father Sullivan who visited her tent regularly whenever the circus was in Chicago. "And Father doesn't exactly come to my tent to pray," she'd add, "although he gets down on his knees a lot." And she'd laugh her unfiltered three-pack-a-day laugh.

Ronnie realized soon enough that he hadn't exactly fallen for the Virgin Mary but he was still hooked. There was something appealing about a woman who was up front, or maybe it simply had to do with Carmelita taming snakes. You had to be vigilant for that kind of job, you had to calculate the risks and prepare yourself for the unexpected. There was something damn attractive about a woman who would do that, and once you got to know her better you could tell she'd once been a dreamer. People who joined the circus usually were. But now she was merely practical. People who stay with the circus usually are. Nothing ever surprised her. Perhaps that's why she went along when my father and his friends explained Ronnie's dilemma. Sure she would see him in her trailer after the show on Saturday night. But he would have to wait until after clean-up because everybody had to help dismantle the tents, since the circus was leaving at day-break Sunday morning.

"Where will the snakes be?" my father asked.

"In their box under the bed," answered Carmelita.

But not to worry, they would be so tired they wouldn't budge. Ronnie wouldn't even know they were there.

It hadn't occurred to anyone up to that very moment that the snakes would be in Carmelita's trailer. They all knew how terrified Ronnie was of snakes, and they did have Ronnie's best interests at heart, but the temptation was too great. Five minutes before Ronnie was due at the trailer, my father, fortified by his twelve-ounce flask, snuck into Carmelita's trailer and grabbed Sully by each end and placed it under the covers at the foot of Carmelita's bed. It hardly stirred. It was so tame it just curled up and went on sleeping. Then my father went to meet Ronnie and walked with him to Carmelita's trailer for support. "What can I tell you," my father always says at this point in his story. Ronnie wasn't in there five minutes before he yanked the door open and bolted out of the trailer wearing nothing but an unbuttoned shirt, clutching his pants in his hands.

He was running across the lot, stepping in elephant shit, cursing like you've never heard, when who should walk by, lurking to see what the freaks of nature were up to on their last Saturday night in town? None other than Billy Sunday.

By this time the Enchantress wasn't the only one perched on the step of her trailer, yelling to Ronnie that he'd scared Sully half to death, calling him and his friends perverts. Standing at the doors of their trailers was the most extraordinary assortment of human beings, in various states of undress—the Tattooed Marvel; Tom Thumb II and his wife; the Fat Lady; the Bearded Lady; the Tallest Man on Earth; Frog-Woman; Ape-Man; Mossa Singhalee; the Flying Dutchman—all of them cheering while Ronnie, still clutching his pants, stood there, cursing his friends, the snake, and the Enchantress.

Billy Sunday's face wouldn't have looked more stricken if he'd wandered into hell. Unaware, poor bastard, that he'd come as close to paradise as anyone could get. But that's another story.

CARNAL KNOWLEDGE

For a period of several months during her third year, the young girl is practically unable to eat. The first year was difficult enough, the food unfamiliar, tasteless, but she resigned herself. Now everything is repulsive: the stringy meat, the watery vegetables, the warm milk that forms a skin and sticks to her lips, the tapioca pudding with the glutinous lumps. Even the taste of the Eucharist each morning nauseates her, the thin wafer made flesh, made bloody on her tongue before it dislodges from her palate, scrapes down her throat, along her stomach wall, towards the rot of her bowels. Each morning, as she kneels at the balustrade before crisp linen and lace and her eyes lift towards the perfumed hand blessing her face, she wonders what morsel of Christ's body she is about to ingest. Which organ, limb, entrails, or wound. Which mucus, marrow, semen.

It began the night she refused to eat her portion of boiled pork liver. Amid the rattling of knives, forks, and spoons and the droning voice reading an epistle or lesson, she noticed the listless manner in which all the girls chewed their food. Every night, except for the sound of utensils and chewing, supper proceeded in silence, each girl watching the others masticate, each face displaying the misery of not being able to communicate her revulsion. Until she simply said no, I will not eat this piece of boiled pork liver. No. I will not eat it no matter how long I have to perch on this refectory stool.

At first the threats from Soeur were uncompromising. We'll stay here all night if we have to. Sit with your back straight. But after three or four hours it was obvious nothing would induce the young girl to give in to the congealed greyness on her plate. Not even threats of waking Mère. Finally the pleas turned to reasoning. You must eat to maintain your strength. The equation was too familiar. If what the priest had said was true, about wine turning into blood and bread into flesh, then nothing good could evolve from this dead meat. She could even turn into a pig.

The first year, after recovering from the shock of being away from home, she relinquished all power over her own small life. There was nothing to do but yield to God's representatives, the nuns, day in and day out. No choice, no voice, no say. But she had discovered one area where she could exercise a certain degree of control. No one could force her to eat what she didn't want to. To put that piece of boiled pig in her body would have meant surrender.

Perched on her stool, alone in the refectory, she filled the hours by whispering the names of her parents, the names of her friends back home, the streets they lived on, the schools they went to, the food her mother prepared. Blood sausage, *du boudin,* as black and swollen as its name. She visualized the blood of the chickens her mother killed because they were cheaper that way: the cutting off of the head, the plucking and evisceration, the yellow foot with its elegant nails, the tendon carefully stripped so that when she pulled on it, the foot opened and closed like a claw. She imagined the delicate birds of her dreams that fed on the fragrance of flowers. Back straight, she sat on her *tabouret* until Mère finally burst into the refectory at two in the morning, face red with fury, and ordered her to bed.

Since that incident she's barely been able to eat anything, in spite of Soeur Richard, who's in charge of the infirmary, warning her that she's losing too much weight. "If you don't eat, you'll have to be confined to the infirmary and fed intravenously," Soeur cautions. But to eat would mean giving in to the craving and longing she felt during most of that first year.

Every morning immediately after breakfast each girl completes the chore she was assigned at the beginning of the term. The young girl is familiar with most of them: refectory consists of cleaning and washing up after meals; hallways means sweeping and dusting and removing the scuff marks on the floors, baseboards, and stairs, except for once a month when the long stretches of dark linoleum have to be washed, waxed, and polished. Parlour duties are always coveted since the room is seldom used except by Father Thériault, who eats breakfast in the small room off the main parlour every morning after mass. Father Thériault is tall and has dark wavy hair like Robert Taylor.

Dormitories are the worst chores, the sinks often plugged with hair and the toilets stained yellow and brown, but even they aren't as offensive as the infirmary. Infirmary used to be the most popular because of the illustrations in the medical books, but that was before Soeur Richard. Before word got out about Soeur's peculiar habit of giving almost every girl who came near the infirmary an enema, regardless of her symptoms. According to Soeur Richard, the rites of purification are not confined to souls; they affect all parts of the body. "The seed of all physical disease is located in the intestines and communicated to the head, the heart, and the kidneys, as well as all principal organs of the body, through the nerves," she explains as she stands holding a douche bag over the naked body of the young girl lying face down on the bed.

Before the news of Soeur Richard's obsession, almost every girl managed to fake an ailment that would guarantee a few days in the infirmary at least once a year. A few girls learned how to raise their temperature by eating black pepper or holding hot water in their mouths just before Soeur placed the thermometer under their tongues. Others mutilated themselves, cut themselves on an arm or a hand, making sure the wound got infected. One girl carved a cross on her right shoulder and had to be sent to an outside hospital for several weeks.

Before Soeur Richard, a few days in the infirmary not only offered a respite from rules or exams, it also meant access to books not available in the convent library. They were kept under lock and key in a glass-fronted cabinet but everyone knew that the spring lock on the door was not impervious to agile fingers. It was common knowledge that while Soeur was at prayers or some other observance, a tongue depressor at the right angle between the frame and the door would release the lock. The cabinet held all manner of books on medical science and the human body.

One book listed the correlations between human and animal physiognomy and explained how a person's character could be established from the similarities; another explained how physiological functions were distanced from the soul and why Sainte Catherine bled milk instead of blood when she was decapitated. There was a compilation of miracles performed by the breast milk of the Virgin Mary.

Le Dictionnaire de Théologie rationalized the resurrection of the body after death and the phenomenon of bodily apparitions of saints to simple minds. There was a brief biography of the twin healers Saint Cosmas and Saint Damian, holy medicine men from the East. There were books by a Docteur Charcot in Paris who specialized in the illnesses of women incarcerated at a hospital called La Salpêtrière. One of the books had several photographs of women bearing one of two expressions: the delirious gaze of holy icons or the bewildered look of the perpetually damned.

A few months after the incident of the pork liver, the young girl is confined to the infirmary for two weeks before Christmas holidays. The nuns are very concerned about her weight and Soeur Richard has been advised to give her a special tonic and a diet of fattening foods before she goes home. For the first time at the *pensionnat* she is given thick cream with her porridge, gobs of cheese on the macaroni, and ice-cream after every meal.

Most of the books in the glass-fronted cupboard are French but there is one English book the young girl returns to whenever she can. *Gray's Anatomy.* She understands little of it—medical language is like the language of prayers, codes developed around afflictions—but the pictures of the different parts of the body interest her. A skeleton, she discovers, consists of two hundred bones, and three hundred pages describe all of them in detail, from the cranium to the metatarsal joint of the foot. The drawings of feet are like the patterns she's seen through the machines in shoe stores when she goes shopping with her mother. The delicate white lines that extend between the webs of the toes.

Pages 295 to 455 are on muscles and fasciae—a kind of bandage that keeps everything from spilling out of the body. A shaved head reclining on a block beneath the back of the neck has been skinned, the scalp peeled away and folded in neat corners. In other drawings, incisions run along the entire length of the back from the base of the head to the coccyx, or along the front thorax from the throat to the lower abdomen. There is a section called "muscles of inspiration and expiration", which she reads as "muscles of inspiration and expiation", which doesn't surprise her. Nor is she surprised to discover that several pages have been carefully cut out from the book's spine. The index column indicates that the missing pages, 355 to 375, deal with the *rectus, erector penis, sphincter vaginae,* and *erector clitoridis,* words she jots down to look up later in her dictionary or in the library encyclopedia, although she suspects she knows what they mean.

The section on the vascular system is intact. The position of the heart, its size, its openings. Patterns of vessels and branches. She revels in the names of the nervous system. *Dura mater.* Hard mother. Loses herself within the labyrinths of organs, cochlea, lachrymal canals, but feels thwarted again to discover that pages 1009 to 1023, "The Male Organs of Generation", have also been removed. Except for that brief glimpse of Le Noir the Tailor back home she has never seen the "male organs of generation". The missing section is followed by "The Female Organs of Generation", and she is astonished that these haven't been removed—it couldn't have been an oversight, these things never are—and she's even more astounded by the illustration on page 1025.

It takes her several minutes to realize what she's

looking at. These organs are female, the book claims, but to her they are unfamiliar, foreign. Perhaps this is what Soeur meant when she said apparitions were divine but illustrations were demonic.

At the top of two lobes which the young girl finally recognizes as a behind, there is a small hole labelled *anus* from which extends a halo of hair. Inside the hair are oval shapes framing smaller ovals and more holes. *Orifice of vagina. Orifice of urethra.* Petals tagged *labium* frame the holes and at the top of the petals there's a knob, a *glans clitoris.* Unlike the English words she's had to look up in the dictionary, these carry a trace of recognition, and she knows they will have something to do with her eventually. They are strewn across the page like an inevitable accident, the end result when girls become women.

She once heard senior girls talk about something women have between their legs that resembles a man's penis, but there is no evidence in the illustration of what this could be. The senior girls even said all women wanted a penis, but that was silly. Why would they want anything dangling between their legs? In any event, there is nothing in the illustrations of women's organs resembling what she imagines a penis to be.

The following pages show the interior of the female organs of generation. The vagina extends all the way to a pouch called the uterus. A posterior view of the uterus looks like an octopus, with arms called fallopian tubes and ovarian vessels. A cross-section of an egg-shaped form, an ovary, shows blood-vessels, follicles, membranes, and an ovum. Apparently the ovum escapes from the egg-shaped form along the arms of the octopus until it gets to a main body and attaches itself inside, where it will either become a baby or be discharged.

The young girl feels as if she's been turned inside out. The sensation in her stomach is not unlike what she felt the night she sat on the refectory stool when she wouldn't eat the pork liver, a blend of nausea and horror, although this time the malaise is accompanied by a wave of excitement.

Her hand reaches between her legs. In the privacy of the infirmary, away from Soeur's gaze, she follows the outline of what she looks at in the book while identifying and naming each part grazed by the tip of her finger. She feels hairs she didn't know she had. *Pubis.* The fold inside the hairs must be the *labium.* Another fold. She mustn't look, except for the picture. Looking would be going too far, that would be a sin even more mortal than what she is doing now. In any event what she wants are the words that will describe it all. *Labium minus. Nympha.* Her finger delves into the folds and separates two that have stuck together. *Vestibule.* She probes around for the *Orifice of the vagina* but she finds no orifice, no hole. Perhaps it's like the soul—it's there but it can't be seen. Her finger proceeds to the small knob at the top of the *Labium minus. Prepuce. Glans clitoris.* The words sound like the Latin names in the prayers and litanies she has been made to learn by heart. The more she repeats them, the more they sound like phrases of the holy mass, except that these particular words, she knows, are impious and unlawful. They are no more appropriate within the confines of the infirmary than they would be in a church.

As her finger grazes the clitoris back and forth, she is invaded by the excitement of a new sensation. The words she has just learned occupy her entire being. *Anus. Mons Veneris.* Each one permeated with who she is and will be.

She repeats each new word over again, as if each organ, each appendage, in being named for the first time, has undergone a radical change, a metamorphosis. For the first time in many months she is overcome with boundless exhilaration. In the process of naming parts of her body she didn't know she had, she is unable to find words to describe what she's feeling. She is bewildered by sensations to which she readily submits. A trembling on the verge of fulfilling a secret yearning.

***

Except for cases of severe illness it is against regulations to excuse any girl from morning chores, but because they are alarmed at the amount of weight she's been losing, the nuns have assigned the young girl to the sacristy. It's the most coveted chore, requiring only light sweeping, dusting, folding and putting away vestments. Sometimes Soeur requests that she polish some of the holy objects, the candle holders, the censer, but never the chalice. Only the priest's state of grace allows him to handle the chalice. If anyone else were to touch it, it would be defiled; touching it is a mortal sin.

It never occurs to the young girl to violate that rule until one morning, shortly after being released from the infirmary, and without premeditation, she approaches the small door behind which the chalice and the consecrated hosts are kept. A girl was expelled once after she was caught removing the Eucharist from her mouth, and it caused a scandal. Only a priest can handle the blessed body of Christ, and even then it has to be held between his index finger and thumb.

In nomine Patri.

She opens the door with the gold-plated sun and pulls out the silver and gold chalice. She retrieves a fistful of consecrated wafers and puts them into her mouth.

In nomine Patri.

She is ingesting the body of Christ. She takes another fistful. They feel stiff and sticky in her mouth, adhere to her teeth and palate, and have to be dislodged with the tip of her finger.

In nomine Patri.

She is ingesting divine flesh. The heavenly manna that nourishes bodies and does away with dependence on food and boiled pigs. This bread of angels will restore the strength she has lost and release her from the sadness and guilt that filled her after the incident in the infirmary.

The body of Jesus will cleanse the rot of her bowels. She stuffs more wafers into her mouth. This is the rite through which unworthy daughters swallow the flesh of the Father and make themselves worthy again. Not only the Father's liver but his entire body, so the two of them, daughter and Father, are one.

In nomine Patri.

Her throat feels as narrow as a needle, as if she were choking. Between her index finger and thumb she takes one host from the chalice and places it carefully against her belly, inside the band of her underwear. She will carry it there until her stomach swells. Until something grows inside her.

BABEL NOËL (iii)

The danger in our time is not the Tower of Babel, but making everything into *one*. Making historical, cultural or linguistic diversity into one. . . . It is frightening to consider the power of the English language to eliminate the natural multiplicity of language, for example.

Robert Kroetsch
Labyrinths of Voice

Every Christmas morning when the children were small, I would have to convince them it wasn't time to get up yet, both of them standing by our bed, peering me out of my sleep at four in the morning. Two hours later, the persistent ticking of a clock an inch from my face would waken me again and Louise would assure me Santa had already been.

Now the ritual is reversed, I'm the one who wakes up first. After Geoffrey has lit the fireplace, I summon everyone to the living room for the exchange of presents. Every year Geoffrey swears he will never again give in to the waste, and every year he's as guilty as the rest of us. Only my father seems immune to the excess, partially out of restraint, partially out of indifference.

There is a tradition that requires Catholic children to ask their father to bless them on Christmas morning, and I have a vague memory of having done this at least once. I feel mortified thinking about it now, but it was at a time when convent fervour often extended into the holidays. Even then my father didn't take these religious displays too seriously and, embarrassed but not wanting to humiliate me, he muttered something about his daughter getting a good education and making lots of money so she could take care of him in his old age.

Immediately following the presents and breakfast, my mother disappears into the kitchen. I suggested once, if only for the sake of change, that we prepare something else other than turkey. A roast goose stuffed with chestnut and sausage like the one we'd had when we lived in Paris. But everyone, especially the children, objected. It wouldn't be Christmas without the proverbial turkey prepared according to my mother's recipe. Hours of chopping, measuring, basting, this is her gift to the family.

Christmas dinner is usually spirited but this year it's at its liveliest. When the children were younger, cranky and exhausted from too many sweets and too much activity, they often behaved like weary victims, but now they act like tolerant adults. My father, after two days of persevering mostly in French, has resigned himself to speaking mostly English, either in keeping with the Christmas spirit or because he's tired of having to repeat everything three or four times. It's a familiar pattern, one of resolve giving way to expediency.

"So, David, you haven't told me if you were studying some French at university. . . .

"No, Grandpa, I'm not."

"But you said you were taking . . . how did you say . . . the science of *politiques*. . . ."

"Political science."

"And there are no things French in political science?"

"Well, we study some French issues, but in English."

"Ah . . . some French issues, in English. . . . And why do you study this political science?"

My father's present mood is far from apathetic, and

any questions relating to French and English issues are probably not idle but leading to a collision course. Three or four months ago I would have rushed to David's rescue and diverted the conversation but I'm curious to see if he can handle it. I was very disappointed he didn't take at least one French course at university and I'm curious as to how he's going to justify this to his grandfather.

"Because political issues interest me."

"And you don't think you need the French to know about the politics?"

"No, not really."

"*Bien, mon cher garçon,* without French it's getting harder to get a good job. Everyone is either scrambling to learn a little French or joining the bigoted "English only" ranks these days."

Sensing that his grandfather wants to push the matter further, and not particularly inclined to give him the satisfaction, David shrugs in his usual dismissing manner. "Well, I guess I'll have to join the English only ranks," he quips, and asks for more stuffing.

The subject has gone as far as it should. It threatens the balance I've tried to maintain over the last few days. I am, after all, the hyphen, the third element that provides coherence between my children and my parents and their different languages. We've spent enough holidays together for me to know that, under the circumstances, tradition can only be upheld if we adhere to certain rules. We avoid topics that are too controversial. We try to remain as impartial as possible if conflict does occur. And we compromise. My father, however, cannot forego the opportunity to air something that has, apparently, bothered him for some time. "*Mais David,* don't you think this attitude has caused enough problems for this country?"

It would be best to put an end to this exchange so perhaps David needs me after all. "It's not as simple as all that, it's not just an issue of language. Anyway, I don't think it's the right time to be discussing this." A hint of irritation has crept into my voice and I regret having said anything. It will only add fuel to a potential dispute.

"Of course, it comes down to language," my father exclaims, offended. "And why shouldn't we talk about it? If people respected each other's language and opinions a little more, we wouldn't need government accords and laws and bills to speak to each other."

"Exactly," David pounces. "We shouldn't have laws and bills to protect one language because too many different cultural groups live here now. What about all those people who don't speak French or English? Where are they going to fit in?"

Geoffrey hasn't given the matter much thought, but the choices seem obvious and reasonable to him. "I guess they'll have to do what all immigrants have done. They'll have to choose to live in either English or French communities."

Geoffrey has never had to deal with problems of language, except the year we spent in Montreal at the time of the referendum. Along with his business partners, he'd ranted against the disastrous effect of the Parti Québécois on the province's depressed economy, and his year there had been a disappointing one. He'd been unable to rediscover the charms of the city he'd known as a student at McGill, he'd said, and I'd teased him about that. "You mean when everyone knew their place?" I'd said.

"In that case, we might as well forget about French in Canada," my father tells Geoffrey, shaking his head in a gesture of defeat. "Those immigrants will be assimilated by the English, just like your kids."

My father's accusatory tone is so startling, it takes several seconds for everyone to recover. My mother and I attempt to stare our husbands into some sense of discretion while Louise protests that she hasn't been assimilated at all since she can speak French as well as anyone in the family, or better. Geoffrey hopes her insinuation will go undetected, while I desperately search for something to ease the belligerent mood that has settled over Christmas dinner. David, however, beats me to it.

"My mother," he asserts, "should have spoken French to me when I was a child."

I've often related, more as a joke than anything else, how, as a child, David refused to speak French. When feeding him in his high chair, I would point to utensils and foods, *la cuillère, des carottes*, and he would wave a finger of disapproval in my face. At two years old he was already aware of the divisions language generates. At six he had such a tantrum when we sent him to a French immersion school, away from his friends, that we conceded that it might not be the best thing for him just yet. As a teenager he refused everything French, French books, French films, claiming he hated subtitles. I've often blamed myself for not being more persistent, but I thought I recognized the need for a young son to align himself with his father. I assumed he'd eventually outgrow it.

"That's unfair, David. I tried speaking French in the house but I felt outnumbered."

"Maybe you didn't try hard enough," comes his reply, quick and reproving.

Christine said to me once that speaking French or English to one's children wasn't a matter of choice. French was always more natural to her and she never spontaneously

addressed anyone in English, not even a dog. I attributed
that to the simple fact that she lived in Paris half the year,
but I also realized then the reality of my situation. Most
of my life was lived in English, and French no longer came
naturally to me. I had, for all intended purposes, chosen
the most practical way out. But to be accused of being the
one responsible for David's newly discovered shortcoming
is not only unfair, it's unjust and wounding.

"Well, I suppose if we'd stayed in Montreal and I'd
insisted you attend French schools, not only would you be
able to work for the federal government, you could even
run for prime minister. Sorry I was the one to mess up your
career," I lash out. My composure, my safeguard, has been
eroded. Only my children can reach beyond its veneer and
strip me of its protection.

"Oh, because *you* wanted to stay in Montreal and you
couldn't because of us." It's Louise's turn to defend the role
she may have unwittingly played in her mother's defec-
tion.

"That's right. I didn't feel I had the right to impose
my language and my culture on the rest of the family. We
moved back to Ontario, where you were all very happy to
return to the comfort of one language. *Your* mother
tongue."

"Come on, it wasn't like that at all," Geoffrey offers.
"You didn't like Montreal at the time of the referendum
any more than we did. We were all relieved to get out of
there." He is exasperated, but I'm still smarting and have
no intention of surrendering.

"I was happy to leave because we lost the referendum.
Had we won I would have stayed." The words, barely
uttered, have the effect I was striving for. Everyone stares
in disbelief.

My father, who feels responsible for a situation that's careering towards disaster, is the first to come to the rescue. For the first time in the presence of his son-in-law and on the French-English issue he decides to settle for a truce, which, as far as he's concerned, has nothing to do with compromise.

"We won, we lost, who cares? The important thing is, the French had the opportunity to say what was on their mind and hopefully the rest of Canada listened. We all have to give and take. Look at me, I'm putting these damn little red English berries on my turkey and, you know, I don't mind it. All these years I didn't know what I was missing."

Unfortunately, his attempt at a truce isn't as meaningful to his son-in-law as he hoped. A disturbing element has surfaced, and now that it's been brought out in the open, Geoffrey isn't about to dismiss it.

"What do you mean, you would have stayed in Montreal? There was never any question of us staying in Montreal."

"There was never any question of *you* staying in Montreal, but I was excited by the events: the prospect of a language, a country I could call my own. Hear my children speak *my* language."

"Oh, give it up, Laura, you're not even from Quebec, you're from Ontario. You were born in Ontario, you've spent most of your life in Ontario, and let's face it, you speak English better than you speak French." Geoffrey's tone is incredulous, dismayed.

"I wouldn't have stayed in Montreal!" Louise exclaims, horrified at the thought. "I would have come back here with Daddy! I can't believe you would even think of splitting the family because of some stupid political problem that has nothing to do with us!"

"Oh for God's sake Louise, I'm here aren't I?" Once again I feel outnumbered. Once again I yield to the inevitable. If the scission, the split that exists between my children, my parents and myself because of language, cannot be mended, it must, for the sake of the holidays, be turned inward once again. We are, after all, family, and Christmas is the word made flesh.

In any event I probably wouldn't have stayed in Montreal, but there was exhilaration at the thought of rediscovering a lineage, a first language. If you can hold on to that, everything follows. The elation I'd experienced had been so pervasive, so innate, it had exceeded other priorities. For a few weeks I had inwardly, proudly, carried my own banner.

Then, for a long time after the referendum, there was the feeling that I didn't belong, but when I asked myself what it was I no longer belonged to, there was no clear answer. Should language account for everything? It almost never said what you wanted to say anyway. Whatever language I've spoken has never been right. At the convent I'd been forced to speak differently from my parents, the French the nuns insisted upon was almost a second language. In Paris it had been a different French again. No matter how you spoke it, Canadian French was never good enough. Until I'd mastered English, no language was ever adequate. With Geoffrey, at the university, and at work, I had adapted my colours to my surroundings, as protection but also to please.

My mother is the first to break the deadlock. "Anyway, *David,* it's not too late to learn another language, especially at your age. It should be your responsibility now, not your mother's. So . . . who wants more turkey and stuffing?" she offers as a digression and my father is only too happy to leap at the chance.

"Sure, get the rest of the turkey from the oven, I could use some more."

But my mother hasn't forgiven him for starting the whole mess in the first place. "Is your ass glued to your chair?" she shoots back, glaring at my father, and everyone laughs, relieved and grateful for her perfect timing.

ACHILLES' HEEL

Is it the sudden realization that a tradition is about to end that makes us want to forge history? "Your mother and I are getting too old to travel at Christmas, you'll have to get used to our not coming every year," my father warns me. He hates airplanes and trains, hasn't been feeling well lately, so this may indeed be the last time they travel the four hundred miles. Is it the shift that time imposes that makes me want to retrace my steps and shield my past against dissolution?

As my father and I sit in the TV room after everyone else has gone to bed, spent from an unusually animated and emotional Christmas dinner, I ask him about his childhood and when he was a young man. Much of what I know of the lives of my parents has been passed on in the form of stories revised over the years, tall tales that grow taller as they spin themselves into the spine of my history, each tale an acoustic mirror reflecting the different facets of my background, my geography.

After several years of an impertinent stance towards fathers in general, I urgently need to hear my father's stories again and displace the anger that reinforces the power we assign to all men, a power my father has never possessed. In any event, a father's stories shouldn't diminish a daughter's voice. On the contrary, they should allow conversation to open between them as they establish their proximity and their differences.

Although he loves to joke when he's with friends, with his family my father can be very reticent. "Your Achilles' heel," I tease, but references not immediately understood only make him feel more uncomfortable, so I resolve to interrupt as little as I can.

When I told Madame Wickersham that my father's name was Achilles and his stepfather's was Hector, she said such coincidences shouldn't be overlooked. She brought me Homer's *Iliad* and several books on mythology and suggested that I write about my father as a mythological character. Private experience always echoes collective memory, she said, although I had no idea what she meant at the time. *The name of my father,* the story began, *means river, and rivers are the ancestors of the oldest of tribes and heroes. My father's name is Achilles.* Madame must have realized that I'd stolen most of the material from the books she'd lent me, but she didn't mention it and she read my story to the class.

Four months before he was born, Achilles' father died and Achilles fell from the heavens like rain.

"How did your father really die? Was it pneumonia or tuberculosis?" I ask my father.

"As you know, he died four months before I was born, when he was thirty-two years old, so I didn't know him. Some people said he died of tuberculosis because it was very common at the time but others claimed he had contracted pneumonia after his sled and horses broke through the ice while crossing Lake Temiskaming. *Mon oncle* Ti-Roc said the pneumonia never cleared up, and having to work the land that spring made it worse.

"I only got to know him through these various versions, the way death has of changing everything into legend, transforming the dead into heroes like movie stars. The first time I saw Tom Mix handling horses in *Riders of the Purple Sage*, I knew my father had been just like him.

"So there was my poor mother, twenty-eight years old, four children and another one on the way, and no husband. They say she did her best to look after us but I guess a small farming community like St-Bruno-de-Guigue didn't offer young widows too many opportunities. After I was born she got a job working in the kitchen in the sanatorium in Haileybury but she'd heard rumours about a boom town farther north. Endless veins of gold running through the earth all the way from Dawson City to South Porcupine, a few hundred miles north of Haileybury. So she placed the five of us in different homes around St-Bruno, left for South Porcupine, and found a job in the kitchen of the local hotel. I was about eight months old when she left so I don't remember any of this. I know that two of her children, a boy and a girl, died of Spanish fever before she had the chance to see them again, and the rest of us stayed with the families we were placed with until she sent for us five years later. So I didn't see my mother until I was five, and it isn't clear in my mind if what I remember about those five years are truly memories or what I heard as anecdotes. The one thing I do remember is my bewilderment at having to leave the people I'd assumed were my family. My foster parents, I guess you'd call them, often talked about a mother who would eventually return, a real mother. But when you're four or five the concept of an absent mother isn't easily grasped. If anything, it fixes the image of a real mother as someone who is forced to abandon her kids to foreign fevers."

Achilles of the swift feet said, "We must make our way home," but within his breast his heart was divided two ways.

"When my mother remarried, my two sisters and I joined her and her new husband in Timmins because that's where the work was. And everything went smoothly for a while. It was my stepdad's first marriage and he was delighted to inherit a ready-made son. All my life, whenever I've gotten myself into trouble, I've been reminded by my two sisters, or even now by your mother, how my stepdad's lack of discipline is at the root of my flawed character. They claim he sided with me in everything. Brought me bags of candy from his sister's variety store; let me skip school so I could join him and his men and help clear the parcels of land he had contracts for. He could cut trees like Apollo. Within ten years Timmins would have a few thousand houses, hundreds of businesses, a high school, but in 1919 it was barely a trail through the woods, and my stepdad and his men, his four horses and sled, played a big part in the clearing of that land, at least in the beginning. It wasn't long before I thought he was as good a replacement for a real dad as any.

"The five of us lived in a three-room tarpaper house by the Temagami River, a shack, really, and everything was pretty good for the first three years. But then my mother got ill more and more often. She was very thin, which wasn't very fashionable in those days. She sent away for McCoy's Cod Liver tablets from the back of a magazine but they didn't do much good. The ads claimed any woman could get rid of a peaked face and a hollow chest by gaining ten pounds of healthy flesh in thirty days, and my mother would cut the ads out and send away for the tablets, but they didn't change how exhausted she looked.

"The sicker my mother got, the more my stepdad drank. I guess he was an alcoholic. The last year before she died was a vicious circle of my mother getting ill, my stepfather getting drunk, my mother recovering barely enough to look after us and the land-clearing business, making sure the contracts were filled, until she got sick again and my stepdad, who had barely recovered from his last bout, was off on another one. He would work very hard for a few months, then drink nonstop for two or three weeks, until his body gave way to uncontrollable shaking and his mind to monsters so vivid even I could see them. It must sound dramatic but it wasn't all that bad. Children are pretty adaptable I guess. Most kids accept what's around them and don't look for the holes. At least not until they get older.

"Looking back on it later I realized how sick my mother must have been that winter. One Sunday afternoon I went skating on the river behind the house. One of the first things my stepdad had bought me when I came to Timmins was a pair of Starr skates, and I got to be a pretty good skater. The Temagami River separated the town from the other bank, which was still thick with spruce, birch, and pine, a kind of underworld waiting to be broken. That's what everything seemed like in those days, waiting to be broken.

"On Saturday mornings or Sunday afternoons most of the town's children skated the river, ran races, played hockey. As it got darker I would look towards the house to see if the coal-oil lamp was lit, an indication supper would be ready soon. But that afternoon the lamp was never lit and when I returned to the house I was told my mother had gone. She was thirty-eight years old and she had died of tuberculosis ten years after my father."

Young Achilles went and sat in sorrow beside the grey sea, looking out on the infinite water, and the lady his mother heard him and spoke to him: "Why then, child, do you lament? What sorrow has come to your heart now?"

"My stepdad began a drinking spree you wouldn't believe. Lasted until he'd lost his business, the horses and sled, sold all our belongings. Drank until everything and everyone had left him, except the monsters. It was months before anyone saw him sober again. Even then it was never for very long.

"I remember seeing a picture of a totem pole once and thinking how my mother was like the little frog sitting at the top of the totem. The one creature able to live a double life, able to live anywhere and make it feel like home. I didn't know her for very long but that's how I remember her. Nothing was ever too much for her. Like your mother and her mother before her, I suppose."

* * *

"Tell me about when you were a waterboy in the lumber camps. You have so many stories about that."

They said no mortal would dare come to our encampment, not even one strong in youth, but from the age of nine young Achilles lived in the woods at the mouth of a river with beasts, wild and tame.

"Those aren't stories, that's my life," my father replies almost as a protest.

"But how did you come to live in a lumber camp at

nine years old? Why weren't you in town going to school?"
I press, already aware of the answers but wanting to hear
them once more, as if to confirm them before I write them
down. Because he's very self-conscious, my father sometimes speaks as if his mouth were filled with stones, but
tonight, as if he'd been visited by that singular bird whose
beak is a remedy for people whose words fall out of their
mouths too early or too late, he speaks for more than six
hours.

"I couldn't stay in town to go to school because there
was no one there to look after me. After my mother died,
my older sister and her husband took me to a lumber camp
at Big Water Lake where they worked from October to
April. She was ten years older than I was, felt responsible
for me, but there were no handouts, everyone had to pitch
in, so I became the waterboy.

"The first year after my mother died, my sister sent
me to school for a month in September and again when we
moved back into town at the end of April, but I was too far
behind so I stopped going altogether. Which was fine by
me. I'd learned to read as much as a kid learns in three
years.

"My main recollection of school before my mother
died was having to memorize catechism. I have a very clear
memory of that. Hours spent memorizing a lesson, repeating it word for word to my mother just before leaving the
house and forgetting everything the moment I came face
to face with the teacher and the rod. And I was never
spared that rod. Working as a waterboy had its lonely
moments but at least it gave me the illusion of being my
own boss. God and his endless laws and impossible
language couldn't reach me as long as I was protected by
men who cursed, seldom changed their longjohns, and

told stories more spellbinding than any I'd heard in catechism class. God's language never spoke to human beings, at least it never spoke to me, but having to learn all that catechism by heart must have taught me how to read. It wasn't long before I could read my way through French and English magazines.

The very immortals can be moved; their virtue and honour and strength are often greater than the gods.

"My sister was in charge of the cooking, cleaning, and laundering for the twelve men at the camp, and I worked for my room and board but no wages. She was a good cook. Soup, beans, roast. Rabbit stew with salt pork was my favourite. We all lived together in a log cabin twenty by twenty-four feet, seven bunks along one wall, so everyone had to double up to sleep. No mattresses, just a blanket covering some hay and cedar branches against the wooden frames and two blankets to cover ourselves. The cedar branches were important to protect us against head lice.

"It must have been worse for my sister than for myself. Her husband would never have left her on her own in town. He was your strong silent type, twenty-nine years old, and pretty strict with both of us. Used to beat the hell out of my dogs. That was the only thing I ever cried about. Being a waterboy meant getting your own dog-team and sled to fetch the water and run errands. I'd gotten the dogs all trained and trusting but my brother-in-law would turn on them at the slightest excuse and it would take weeks to get them to listen to me again. So scared they just cowered and pissed in the snow when he was around.

"I've read many times how well men looked after their animals in the lumber camps of Northern Ontario, how they spent time grooming their horses, but that's not how I remember it. Horses were pretty expensive so the men had to be careful not to abuse them until they dropped dead, but they were often covered with wounds from a harness that didn't fit or from whipping. One guy got so mad at an old horse once, he hit it in the middle of the forehead with his axe. Killed it right on the spot.

"When a horse died they strung its body up in the trees for dog food, its frozen carcass hanging as if from a gallows, its bewildered stare fixed on you when you rode by in your sled. An eerie sight as it began losing limbs. A carcass covered in white frost like a ghost. Or an angel. Crows and ravens pecking at its flesh until, bit by bit, they'd carried it to heaven."

And a white mare rode the skies.

"I got up every morning at six, half an hour after my sister. After breakfast, I would load up two thirty-five-gallon barrels, harness the dogs to the sled, and ride one and a half miles down the road to Big Water Lake. Took an axe and chisel to cut a hole in the ice. It took about fifteen minutes to get to the lake and about an hour to fill the barrels with a pail. Once the barrels were filled I placed a wet cotton flour sack over the top and circled twine around it so the wet cloth froze, making a cover to keep the water from spilling. By December it was usually forty or forty-five below. At the cabin, the sled, dogs, and barrels were taken inside so my sister could have access to the water, and the dogs could rest and be fed.

"My next chore was bringing in the daily supply of wood for the box stove which was used for both heating and cooking. The cabin was very cold. A shanty, the English called it, because in French it was *une cabane de chantier.* Made of logs caulked with mud and a roof of jackpine planks covered with tarpaper, but the wind whistled right through. At 10:45 I harnessed the dogs again and took the men their lunches, usually bread and salt pork that had come in those thirty-five-gallon barrels we used for water. It was my job to start a campfire for the men to toast their bread, fry the pork, *des grillades,* and biscuits. The biscuits my sister made were very good with molasses. Then I made tea in one-gallon pails that had contained molasses. This is how I learned to be frugal, I guess. Nothing was ever thrown away.

"In the afternoon I sometimes went back for water, always checked my snares for rabbit and hare, and a couple of times a week I went for groceries at Shankman's, about ten miles from camp. Going to Shankman's was a full afternoon's work but the dogs really liked the run through the woods and so did I. At first I was scared but after they killed the horse its ghost came with me everywhere. Scared off wendigos and *loups-garous.* Frightful creatures. The scream of a wendigo as it attacks its prey will paralyse anyone, white or Indian. It'll eat anything but it prefers human flesh. There were stories about how a wendigo had destroyed an entire village at Ghost Point, near Sandy Lake, and although that was way across the other side of the province we knew a wendigo always travelled a straight line, and how fast. Same thing with the *loup-garou.* Another devilish creature, always transforming itself into a wolf or a human being so you never knew what it really was until it was too late. I usually knew if a *loup-garou* was lurking around, though; could feel its eyes on me until it got too close, then the white mare would take charge; she'd hitch me and the dogs to her tail and move like a gust of wind, outdistancing any wendigo or *loup-garou,* so we always made it back safely to the shanty."

* * *

What I write down as my father speaks are not exactly his words, nor are they the distillation of what he tells me. There are several elements that separate his story from fact, the main one being language. The only tongue that could tell my parents' stories is the tongue I have all but lost, a language as depleted as if on a winter's morning, cut off at its source, it had simply withered in my mouth. Cut off from memory, from the slumber of childhood, I cultivated my second language until it replaced my first. As he speaks to me in French, the words, as I write them down, transform themselves into English. Not only do I translate his telling into writing, his history into fiction, but his language into another language. From my father's point of view his version is more accurate in its relation to the past, while from my point of view my version is an advance on the future.

Perhaps this is the writer's function, or the daughter's role. The denial of a family history as simple reconstruction, each translation a facet in the endless possibilities of a story or a life; each interpretation one of the many directions a member of a family might take. The writer as alchemist, practising the arcane art of transmuting elements of reality into the shining, enduring element of fiction. The daughter practising the magical art of transfiguration.

Because my father can barely write he has always thought himself illiterate, but he's far from being unlearned.

"Learned everything by apprenticeship," he claims, "how to cut lumber by lumber-men, how to diamond-drill by diamond drillers." But for a nine-year-old waterboy working in a lumber camp in Northern Ontario in the twenties, writing must have been harder to pick up. He couldn't learn it through apprenticeship, because none of the men could write, and it remains his foreign language. He left me a note once which I had to decipher as if breaking through an exclusive code. I tried to teach him the basics a few times but our sessions always turned into an occasion for another of his yarns. *Ça me rappelle la fois que* . . . each story accompanied by the grand gestures, the rhythm of tall tales.

I used to think of people who couldn't write as unwritten, without history, but even if my father could write I'm not sure how different a story he'd tell. One thing is certain, he's not without history, nor is he uninformed. His favourite Christmas presents have always been books. As he charts his way through biographies, history books, his mouth articulating each word, as if speaking to himself, he painstakingly memorizes facts—the result, perhaps, of an oral culture in which details had to be committed to memory because they didn't exist anywhere else. As his words spill past Christmas night, it's clear that they are also a coming into memory, each story a commemoration, a repetition, in the same way that Christmas commemorates and repeats its myth.

"You never really had a time of childhood."

"A lumber camp isn't all that bad a place for a boy to grow up, the men were always good to me. They expected hard work from everyone and I wanted to please them but they never mistreated me.

"Mostly, I loved riding my dogsled, but I also liked

the stories the men were always telling each other. Even then, I knew that sitting around the coaloil lamp every evening was not an arbitrary gesture. Some men were really quick with punchlines, others were masters of yarns spun over several nights like those serials before movies on Saturday afternoons. I don't know where the stories came from, but these men were never lost for words. Always ready with a smartass comeback. Sometimes the men played cards while someone played the mouth-organ, but most nights, from about six to nine, we settled around the table as soon as it was cleared. The men who didn't like being idle too long fashioned axes handles out of ironwood or sharpened the blades of their axe while they listened. Winter was the best time for storytelling since the spirits were asleep and there was less danger of offending them, although I imagine we offended plenty. The more imagination a storyteller had, the more he played around with facts. I was all ears. As the cabin filled with the scent of kerosene and tobacco, we all grew silent as the appointed storyteller took a few minutes to compose himself, refill his pipe, or roll a new stack of cigarettes. As if waiting, listening to the place where the stories came from.

"There was one man with a long white beard, Robert Chénier, who could spin a tale over several weeks. Made it up as he went along but it always sounded true. Of course some of them were true, such as the stories about the fires that had ravaged the north in 1911 and in 1916. Every oldtimer had something to say about that.

"Our lumber was sold mainly as firewood because it was small. The trees around Big Water Lake had been wiped out by one of those forest fires about ten years before. It was usually impossible to know which year a particular story was about, 1911 or 1916, but it didn't matter. A fire is a fire.

"Chénier described fireballs the size of trees travelling through the air, and how at first people assumed they were just outsized *feux-follets*, and they began sticking needles in trees because it was believed that if a community or a person was attacked by a *feu-follet*, a needle driven into the bark of a tree would force the angry spirit through the eye of the needle, causing it to extinguish itself before the tree burned down. But this time the needles didn't help. The fireballs would explode as soon as they hit their targets, starting more fires, spreading them for miles around. This happened when gold was being discovered all around Timmins, and some people assumed this had something to do with the fires. Some of the foreigners who had experience in these things said that eventually gold seeks revenge on those who overmine it, and that it should only be mined after certain rituals, like praying and fasting, but in Northern Ontario no one knew about such things, or if they'd heard of them they were very sceptical. No one knew gold had a soul.

"The way Chénier described them, the fires were pretty gruesome. People had to leave their homes; some were put into freight cars and taken to the river, women and children were placed into boats while the men, clinging to driftwood, waded farther and deeper into the water. Those who'd had the foresight to bring blankets kept them wet, covering as many heads as they could to prevent hair and eyebrows from singeing. I couldn't bear listening to what happened to the horses. Animals don't understand what's going on. Animals and children. Chénier said that some of the horses had been brought to the water's edge but many of them bolted right back into the flames. Horses don't retreat to die, they barge right in.

People, on the other hand, hid in the woods and perished as fire swept through miles of timber.

"When the worst was over, tents were set up and bodies were put in caskets, five or six to a casket because most of the time there was little left but bones. Chénier said entire families were found in root cellars or in railway rock cuts; they smothered when the fire took away the oxygen. Everyone had a relative who'd died and the subject came up over and over again. The true meaning of hell. When someone you know has had his feet burned off because he was too busy rescuing his family to notice that his shoes were on fire. Hell has nothing to do with notions of offending some distant God, hell is personal. One child lost all twenty members of his family. That's hell.

"They say that after it was over the survivors, who hadn't had anything to eat for several days, flocked to where there had been farms and dug up potatoes baked in the ground. The same with chickens and eggs. The chickens were unevenly roasted and the eggs black and rock-hard but it was food.

"As for animal stories, I wish I had wild ones to tell you, the kind you usually read about in books about the Wild North—bears, wolves, whales—but generally life in the camps was pretty tame. The Wild North doesn't really exist; I know, I've lived there. There were some animals, of course, moose, deer, the odd wolf, but they were more scared of us than we were of them. They only became larger than life as the stories gathered speed.

"Ghost stories were my favourite. Souls caught in limbo, unable to rest until they'd paid for their sins, so they were bitter and full of mischief. It wasn't so much that we believed dead people walked around, it was just that they became so alive in the mouths of the storytellers. And I guess I was still pretty superstitious and gullible. If you believed what the priests in town told you, especially about women and the Devil, the rest didn't sound so incredible. Women and the Devil, they went hand in hand. That's how I learned about sex, in the camps. The men were cautious around me and my sister at first but after a while they must have figured a certain amount of knowledge wouldn't do us any harm. And these lumberjacks were pretty virile, so the stories weren't exactly told in the polished language of refined ladies or nuns. Chénier used to say, "Language is like a bird, if it's colourful it's male." When the stacks of cigarettes were gone and the kerosene barely reached the wick, the stories invariably veered towards wives, virtuous unmarried women, unvirtuous married women, mothers, daughters. Everything that went wrong, especially in affairs of the heart, was blamed on women. Like La Corriveau, who had done away with two husbands by pouring melted lead into their ears. The justice system, and this is a true story, decided she should be hanged and exposed in an iron cage on L'île des Sorcières in Quebec. Problem was, she didn't stay there. Trapped in her heavy iron cage, her ghost wandered into Northern Ontario—ghosts don't recognize boundaries like that. Of course she couldn't move as she pleased, couldn't cross rivers and lakes because of the cage, so she clung to the backs of men in revenge. Many of the men in the lumber camps looked as if they had La Corriveau perpetually strapped to their backs.

"What you read about life in the lumber camps in those days is often picturesque but not always accurate. I guess if your name was William Price or James McGill you made the history books, and that's pretty romantic. If you were a prospector like Noah Timmins you got written about. But the other people, the trappers, loggers, miners, we just made the folksy drawings and tales. I'm not saying it was all bad, but it was hard work. Still, they're good memories, for the most part."

When I listen to the stories of my parents I sometimes wonder if, banished from childhood through the loss of one or both parents, a child doesn't experience a sensation of free-falling. I wonder if, realizing that they don't belong anywhere or to anyone, children don't remain strangers to the usual concepts of time, space, even love. As the frontier between them and the stories they hear breaks down, they must place themselves at the centre of each narrative, projecting themselves into their favourite heroes and heroines.

And Achilles grew up to be a wild young man, sometimes real and sometimes imaginary.

JUNE LILAC

The nuns don't feel competent enough to teach English in the senior grades so a lay teacher has been teaching English literature and composition at the *pensionnat* for several years. Madame Wickersham's French, on the other hand, is spoken with a thick accent which she delivers as if it were her due. "*C'est bien, c'est au point*," she declares as she hands back English compositions, her tone sometimes a little condescending. To be to the point. From her very first year at the *pensionnat* the young girl understood the virtues of sharply delineated outlines that didn't conceal too many hidden meanings. Hidden meanings carry a harsh judgement of character, of one's moral fibre.

The young girl has always written her French compositions in words and sentences that are proper and fitting for a convent. They have never extended beyond that, just as convent life never extends beyond convent walls. Even if she senses that something has been reduced for the sake of clarity, she knows it is best to deal in facts for which no explanations need be given, and the nuns approve of that. But the young girl also knows that clarity does not exhaust all possibilities. There is an element that exceeds rules plotted by nuns, priests, and grammar.

English composition as taught by Madame Wickersham

seems less rigid, or perhaps it is Madame who is more flexible, always encouraging the girls "to invent their truths". The girls are very curious about Madame. She is, after all, the only one, except for Father Thériault, whose life is not dictated by convent regulations twenty-four hours a day. But more significant is the fact that, out of a community of two hundred and fifty women and girls, she is the only one who is married. The girls have guessed her age at about fifty and it isn't long before all fifty years are filled with speculation. Sometimes they just ask her. What's your husband like? Is he a teacher too? Is he handsome? Giggle, giggle. Do you have children? Why are you teaching in a convent instead of a regular high school?

There's an aura of secrecy around Madame Wickersham, unspoken reasons why she's been teaching in a Catholic convent for twenty years although everyone suspects she's Protestant, a detail everyone is supposed to overlook. She never speaks about it and the pursed lips with which the nuns avoid the subject is a sure sign that there's more to their silence than meets the eye.

A few particulars have trickled to light over the years but never the full story. Her husband teaches mathematics at a high school. Yes, he's very handsome, which isn't too surprising since Mrs. Wickersham still looks quite pretty and feminine despite her age. She wears colourful handknitted dresses and Morny perfume of different scents: Gardenia, Pink Rose, June Lilac, and Temptation. A regular Garden of Eden. Giggle, giggle. No, they don't have children.

By the time the young girl reaches senior grade, her interest in English literature and composition has mush-roomed into such "an obsession" that Soeur Auguste appoints her the official inspector of all the new English books purchased for or donated to the convent library. Because the Church brings the list of forbidden books, *livres à l'Index*, up to date each year, the nuns know which French titles should be kept from the library; but with English books there is no such list, so it's harder to tell what should be kept away from impressionable young minds. Since the nuns are fully confident that she is in fact one of their own, or is soon to be, they conclude that the English books she's been reading can't have had too much of a detrimental effect. On the other hand, the fact that she has withstood the onslaught of such books as *Wuthering Heights* could be due to her unerring character, and probably serves to confirm in the nuns' minds her suitability for a holy vocation. The young girl's job, then, is to report any vulgarity or material deemed unfit for the other girls. This should be Madame's responsibility, but since Madame is English and Protestant such an important task can't be left entirely to her discretion. Furthermore, Madame intervenes too often and has even complained to Mère that her judgement is questioned by people who are unenlightened in these matters, so of course Madame can't always be trusted. The young girl, realizing the advantages of having full access to the English books in the library, is careful not to jeopardize the privilege. She is quite happy to report, once in a while, a word, a passage, that the nuns would think hazardous to a pubescent mind. Thus the nuns believe they have one of their own on their side, while the young girl not only gets to read anything she wants, but gets to exercise a certain amount of power over the other girls.

Madame is in fact the only teacher qualified or patient enough to advise the senior classes about books and literature. She's the only one willing to spend time after school discussing novels, poems, or stories, and often hints that she once wrote herself. When asked why she hasn't pursued writing as a career she grows silent, as if she can't bear to repeat an event whose ending is destined always to be the same.

"But you could be a writer if you wanted to," she often tells the young girl. "I like your stories about iron horses, false prophets, and boas. That's what's so exciting about stories, they transform anything or anyone into how you want to see them. I'll bring you a book by an author I've just discovered. A story about a young man who wakes up one morning and finds himself transformed into a man-sized insect. There exist possibilities far beyond the obvious.

"Of course, being a woman and a writer is not easy, you have to be headstrong and even then someone will probably get to you one way or another. George Eliot was right, women's hearts and minds have to be squeezed small like Chinese feet. She was a good writer but she still had to change her name, didn't she? Have you read *Silas Marner* yet? And Virginia Woolf. So much talent but she still drowned herself, didn't she? Walked into a river. A room of one's own, indeed."

Madame knows that Christine and I are best friends and offers more or less the same advice to Christine, except with her she replaces the word "writer" with "painter".

"Whatever you do," she warns us over and over again, "don't ever become a teacher. Being a woman teacher isn't any easier than being a writer or a painter. And don't ever go into teaching for the public school system, it's more confining than being a nun. No advancement, no prestige. The butt of endless jokes, especially if you teach boys. Men teachers and principals will support the boys because supposedly women can't possibly understand the precious little things. I had one male supervisor tell me once that women were inherently dull and cunning, duplicity being one of our evolutionary residues. Imagine! A woman teacher has no rights. If she gets caught questioning a supervisor, or speaking her own mind, she'll soon be looking for another job." Since Madame often went off on one of these tangents, and since they invariably ended with the last comment, we presumed that she was teaching English in a French Catholic convent in a small town because she had at some time questioned a supervisor or spoken her own mind.

When the nuns dressed her up in one of their habits the year she was to graduate, and paraded her from class to class taking pictures, the young girl understood their expectations. The idea wasn't new. She'd heard often enough how some girls wouldn't make it on the outside and would only earn their salvation by joining a holy order. The choice was simple. To become a nun or lose her soul.

It's difficult for a young girl to come to any knowledge of herself in a community as rigid as a convent. There are only two sources on which to draw—her inner sense and the people around her—and the young girl grew distrustful of both. The nuns held all the cards, so the girls learned very early how to please. Decked out in a holy habit, the object of the nuns' admiration, the young girl suddenly acquired a sense of certainty. In the long shapeless dress, her head in a wimple, she occupied another order which had nothing to do with the pettiness and divisions of her daily life. The habit transformed her into something other than a powerless and fearful young girl.

In any event there was no choice. On the outside, she would always be surrounded by temptation. Her parents' hotel. The parking lot. Mike One-Arm's. Le Noir. Her uncle Al, who pawed his nieces every chance he got and who had even managed to get his hands into her pyjama bottoms once when he thought she was asleep. The outside was corrosive, its influence capable of eroding even the strictest convent upbringing. She would have to take the veil. But she didn't want to be an ordinary nun. In her graduating year, before coming home for the Christmas holidays, she wrote home and warned her parents not to buy her any presents because, the following August, she would join an order that sent its members to a special mission in China, and she would therefore have no need of material possessions. Les Filles de la Sagesse would have preferred that she join their holy order but, *faute de mieux,* they were delighted.

She was surprised when her parents didn't say anything about her vocation when she got home. It had been such a momentous decision on her part, she had expected a flurry of comments and questions; but they acted as if she'd never mentioned it in her letters. She was puzzled at first but after two or three days home she was relieved, especially on Christmas morning. The usual presents were waiting under the tree. Perfume, Evening in Paris, in a midnight-blue glass bottle, and bubble bath of the same scent. Books and records, a pair of skates, an angora sweater with a matching tam and gloves. The presents were perfect. The day before, she'd spotted her true love at the skating arena—or, as she later related to Christine, she had met her Heathcliff, except that his name was Geoffrey. He played defence for the Abitibi Eskimos, the hockey team her father sponsored. Number 4. He was English, an

engineer, and he lived with his family in one of the fancy
company houses in Iroquois Falls. Almost every night he
came to the Union Hotel, and she spent the holidays
watching for him from her bedroom window.

The nuns knew immediately. From the moment she
returned to the *pensionnat,* they understood that she was
no longer one of them, no longer part of their strategy.
They observed her out of the corners of their eyes, commented on almost everything she did or said. "You have
reverted to rebellion again, young lady." "Did someone
turn you from your vocation over the holidays?" "Perhaps
you need a retreat, to follow a novena." No, no more
retreats, the young woman resolved, no more days spent in
silence feeling guilty and abandoned.

When it had become clear, that first year, that she
would be staying at the convent for a long time, she'd asked
her mother if they could write their letters in English.
Most of the nuns spoke it badly, and if nothing else the
letters gave her the impression that she could evade their
scrutiny. She often spent free study time copying definitions from her English dictionary, and Soeur, who watched
her over her shoulder, asked why. "I want to be an English
writer," the young girl replied.

"All these words are useless, God is your only witness
and he already knows what you have to say."

But she didn't know what she had to say. She had to
find the words that would tell her. "Curiosity, vanity,"
Soeur said, shrugging her shoulders. The alienation was
not new. Soeur had once warned the seventh grade that it
harboured a bad seed, and she had fixed her eyes upon the
young girl. She had doubled her fervour then. Said twice
as many prayers, gone to confession at every opportunity.

She had reacted as any child under pressure would, the object of adult judgement and prohibition. But she wasn't all bad, she knew better than that, and she would have to take a chance. Even if it meant risking her soul. She wanted an end to all the years of silence. She wanted the taste of words in her mouth as after a novena or a long fast. She yearned for unfamiliar sounds twisting around her tongue as they took shape between her teeth, as they took shape on a page and grew into words, into sentences, into people. She yearned to fill the blank page of her memory.

"Such a perverse pastime," Soeur had said, shaking her head.

> **pervert** from F *pervers per* through or by means of *vers* a line of writing; or L *vertere* to turn; n. one who has turned to error, especially in religion; opposed to convert; v.t. to turn another way; to turn from truth; to divert from a right use; to lead astray; to misinterpret designedly.

At the ceremony on graduation day, Madame sat on stage with Mère and the teaching nuns, all of them taking turns handing out diplomas, awards, and the appropriate "vocation ribbon". Before each graduate left the stage she had to choose a ribbon in one of four satin colours. The white ribbon, the purest and most significant, meant the graduate had chosen the highest calling of all. It was not uncommon for a third of the graduating class to enter a convent.

The nuns usually knew beforehand which girls would choose a white ribbon, but to their delight there was always one girl, sometimes two, who held out until the graduation ceremony to make her sacred calling known, a display the girls viewed with scepticism. Nevertheless, it added an element of suspense and excitement to the graduation ceremony, and the young girl sensed that the nuns were still hoping she would choose white.

It was tempting if only for the drama. Both she and Christine had entertained the idea of picking white to create a sensation, but Christine relented and chose red because it was her favourite colour. The banality of choosing as mundane a colour as green for secretary, blue for teaching, red for nursing, was displaced only by the relief of being able to leave the *pensionnat* at last. In any case it was common knowledge that if you didn't choose white it was just a matter of time until you got married, so the colour didn't matter anyway. As the young girl came face to face with Madame, she knew that if she chose white Madame would see through the charade. There was no colour for becoming a writer so, in spite of Madame's warnings, she chose a blue ribbon, if only for the sake of choosing, and noticed a faint smile cross Madame's face.

As she handed the young girl first prize for English composition, Madame leaned over and embraced her, a gesture she'd never seen in all her years of attending graduation ceremonies. The first prize for composition was usually two books chosen by the teacher, but as the young girl changed the tassel on her mortarboard to the other side to confirm that she was now a graduate, Madame handed her another present, a tubular package wrapped in gift paper, and whispered that she should unwrap it only when she got home.

* * *

In the back seat of my father's new-model Chrysler, retracing my way home from Sturgeon Falls for the last time, I tore open the gift wrap around the two books Madame had given me. One was a copy of Kafka's *Metamorphosis*, and the other was Ovid's *Metamorphoses*, an encyclopedia of myths whose central theme is the incessant reshaping of different forms of life. I was not to understand until much later the significance of those two books, to my life and to my writing.

I opened the tubular package next. It consisted of two magazines, two *Maclean's*, their covers and pages discoloured with age. I turned to a marker inside the first, to an article titled, "Is the School-Marm a Menace?" On the next line, the subtitle read, "The woman schoolteacher constitutes a fundamental weakness in our educational system." The editor noted that the writer of the article, a Mr. Arthur Woollacott, was a school supervisor and principal about to retire.

Although I've returned to these articles several times over the years, they never cease to amaze me, especially as their content has become more relevant to my understanding of how women in education are often perceived. However, to a seventeen-year-old the vocabulary and issues were largely puzzling. I had no idea, for example, what Mr. Woollacott meant by "an east wind is blowing through a jerry-built edifice with foundations of dry rot". What was a jerry-built edifice, and why were its foundations rotting? It became apparent as I read on, that Mr. Woollacott was very unhappy with the educational system in which he was a principal. As much as the system had "mothered" its students in the past, it was now overcome by contemptibly poor schooling and inertia, because no one dared to place the onus on the weakest feature in the system—the woman teacher.

According to Mr. Woollacott, two main factors shaped the Canadian educational system—the inexhaustible wealth of our country's natural resources and the pioneer's wistful leaning towards learning. Successive generations had been nurtured in schools that boasted as formal and academic a discipline as those in Europe, except for one important difference: European schools were staffed by mature men whereas Canadian schools were mostly staffed by young women. Not that his "sisters" could be charged with any specific sinister purpose, but an army of young women little more than children themselves, equipped with less than a modern high-school education, had taken over the field. They had made this sacred vocation their own partly to get away from distasteful household duties but mostly because it gave them a greater chance to land a man a cut above the "village swain", the average male principal or supervisor was apparently very susceptible to feminine wiles. Furthermore, Mr. Woollacott was not the only person of the opinion that women were "a hindrance to our national development"—it was the consensus of all superintendents and inspectors, as well as other men who were in positions to know.

As I read the article, and each time I've read it since, I was reminded of the only pioneers I'd known, my grandparents and my parents. While I never knew my grandmothers personally, the images I have of them, and of my mother, are of average women who led average lives during normal pioneer times.

It was even more difficult to reconcile my grandmothers with the portrait of women who "depreciated anything that stood in the way of money-getting and snaring wealthy husbands so they could lead lives of ease and social prestige." Woman's duplicity was, after all, an inherent evolutionary residue.

The Canadian educational system would do well to heed European schools, Mr. Woollacott advised. With the structure of the German nation shattered by war, the male teachers of that country had found an opportunity to sweep away with one stroke the school organization and replace it with a higher type of citizenship moulded by teachers of a fundamentally different training. Was it any wonder that our boys held no respect for the female teacher? They were demoralized, their need for hero worship frustrated to the point where they sought substitutes in men like Billy the Kid or Al Capone.

I couldn't imagine what this article had to do with Madame or why she had given it to me. Mr. Woollacott was clearly a fossil with no relation to reality whatsoever. I opened the second magazine, which also held a marker, and in letters even bolder than those of the first article the heading read, "REPLY TO MR. WOOLLACOTT BY A WOMAN SCHOOLTEACHER." This was followed by a warning that the author of the article was a class supervisor in a Toronto school whose identity was concealed for obvious reasons.

"A couple of weeks ago," the article began, "a gentle-man named Woollacott exploded with a loud pop in these pages, in a frantic attempt to pin our current political and economic distress directly on women schoolteachers. Waving a crotchety finger, he professed to see a composite picture in which women teachers appear as immature, poorly trained, uncultured, inexperienced girls shirking housework for the easy hours and big pay of teaching; girls who are really looking for a husband, and are loath to accept responsibilities or study for their job a minute longer than the law requires. For many years now teachers have been such handy targets for abuse that we feel Misanthrope Woollacott's inept fling provides a timely opportunity to disclose a few of the actual facts."

The article, evocative of Madame's voice, went on to point out that the "young girls" he referred to were usually mature several years before their male colleagues, certainly equally trained, and generally more experienced in handling children, since most of them had shouldered the responsibility of supervising younger brothers and sisters in the home. If they indeed lacked an element of the male "cultural" background such as "surreptitious exploits in back alleys and lumberyards", they often compensated for this with supplementary courses. These were attended by far more women than men, and if anyone cared to challenge this fact, the anonymous schoolmarm would be delighted to provide the figures to prove it.

"Furthermore, even a dullard would realize that by going into teaching a woman does not escape housework as sociologist Woollacott declaims since she virtually becomes a housekeeper all day long for a half hundred ill-assorted children. What mother would like that job? Most, indeed, breathe a sigh of relief when their own two offspring slam the front door, schoolward bound.

"As for entering the teaching profession mainly to stalk a high-class mate, young women realize soon enough that it is the poorest hunting ground in the world. The average man teacher, in his long crawl to principalship, is long since married.

"Given that Mr. Woollacott sees women teachers as so cleverly ingenious, is it not surprising that he also finds them unsympathetic towards growing boys? The ebullient boy who expects to deceive the teacher simply because she is a woman must be dumbly surprised when she takes him to task because she understands him only too well. Exactly where does statistician Woollacott get his figures when he claims that the causes of increasing crime can be traced to our school system with its preponderance of female teachers?

"Mr. Woollacott crows that men-taught children would be more rugged and individualistic and in a better position to cope with economic and social changes. To clinch this argument, he advances the fact that all schools in Germany are now staffed by mature and trained men. At this blow, we are finally forced to consider that perhaps Führer Woollacott is right. Men could probably trounce children harder and with more permanent effect. Indeed, the more one thinks about it, the more it would seem a good idea if Canada's standing army could be spared from their duty to take spells in the classroom. The children would wax more rugged, and could probably benefit by the individualism of bayonet drill at recess.

"Reformer Woollacott has naively confessed that teacher-training is the responsibility of educational authorities who seemingly don't know what to do about a system that is gently sagging into a moribund state. It is decidedly high time that somebody realized that this system trains our teachers only to strangle them immediately with petty, political red tape. It is also high time that a few zealots, who imagine themselves educators by some divine dispensation of the gods, learn whereof they speak. It must be remembered that our provincial governments decide what shall and shall not be taught in the schools, and scrupulously train the teachers how to do it.

"School boards variously interpret the government's

wise pronouncements, select their own teachers, then saddle them from the start with their regulations. The principals—with a political eye on capricious Home and School associations—then superimpose their personalities on the picture by devising further local rules of procedure and conduct. Teachers have about as much private life as a canary. They must be exemplary of conduct and zealous of routine, for they have more cavilling, critical bosses than any other profession in the world. But let one sincere teacher be caught properly appraising any one of these bosses and she will soon be looking for another job."

Was Madame the anonymous schoolmarm, I wondered. Did it matter? At the end of the schoolmarm's reply to Mr. Woollacott, there were a few words in Madame's hand: "Laura, keep writing. It will bring you much more happiness than being a teacher!" The perfume Madame was wearing at the graduation ceremony had melded with the scent of the old magazines. June Lilac. I never saw Madame again. She wrote a few times asking if I was keeping up with my writing and if Christine was painting, but since I was writing very little and Christine was painting up a storm, I never answered her letters.

BABEL NOËL (iv)

The Christmas dinner has exposed a dilemma for which there is no solution, so no one mentions it again until a few days later, on the morning my parents are about to leave. My mother waits until Geoffrey and the children have left the kitchen, then tells me that my father has something he wants to say.

"I've been thinking about all those things we said at Christmas dinner and there's something I want to add," he says, obviously feeling awkward. Remorse has never been easy for him.

"Well, it occurred to me, given certain situations, that it's best not to think in ways that are too grand. Charity begins at home, as they say. I was thinking of what we said and what it would be like if your mother and I came to visit and the children weren't here because they were spending Christmas with Geoffrey. I don't care how much French or English we speak, Christmas wouldn't be the same without them. Without all of us together. That will happen soon enough, your mother and I are getting pretty old. So all I want to add is that, as far as I'm concerned, you can speak any damn language you want. *Sans récriminations.* That's all I want to say."

I know my father well enough to distinguish between

concession and an attempt to protect what little is left. The thought of losing his grandchildren is more critical to him than his pride. Yet the solution still doesn't seem to me to be that simple.

"But I feel so guilty not speaking more French. Will I always have to lug this guilt around? I'm so sick of it. That's all I ever think about lately, how to retrieve my language, my heritage." There is a mewling to my voice that irritates me.

"Oh, you know, heritage, language, they're not lifeless; they follow the changes of people's lives. For better and for worse your life changed. You have to accept that." For my mother the solution is practical, uncomplicated, and not worth any anguish.

"The thought of living in Montreal felt so right. The possibility was so exhilarating, but now it's as if I've given up. So many of our relatives have given up."

"Living in Montreal isn't going to retrieve your past. As Geoffrey said at the Christmas dinner, you're from Ontario, not Quebec. And you're bilingual. This family is bilingual, and in Ontario that means you end up speaking English most of the time. Especially in Toronto," my mother adds, as if to remind me of my circumstances. "People trying to relive the past, fighting to keep their language, are fighting for time, and that's good. *Le langage c'est un peu comme un miroir,* so of course we would rather it didn't die. But like everything else, language is something that's alive, so it changes."

"If it weren't for the two of you I wouldn't have roots." I want them to understand that without them, when they are no longer around, I will lose one of the few opportunities I have to speak French, but the implication of their advancing age is not something I want to articulate just then. "My past will be confiscated . . . ," is all I can bring myself to say.

"*Ma pauvre Laure, l'arbre n'a pas que des racines, il faut le voir en entier.* Look at the whole tree. *Pis les gens ont des pieds et des jambes,* they move around. We keep looking for roots that never move but that's not how life works. Your life is always on the move, always changing. You opened yourself to another language, there's nothing wrong with that."

"It feels wrong. Like being caught between the devil and the deep blue sea. *Entre l'enclume et le marteau.*"

"*Mais non! Faut pas le voir comme ça!*

"And the children. There are whole parts of our lives, our past, that will always be foreign to them."

"And there are parts of us that will always be foreign to you," my father says, "just as there are parts of the lives of our own parents we never knew or understood. Part of your life as well. That's the way it is with children and parents. Nothing stays the same. Northern Ontario is no longer the same. The Abitibi pulp and paper mill in Iroquois Falls is gradually shutting down. I was reading just the other day that they're going to run out of gold in Timmins by the year 2000. Who would have thought they would run out of gold? Nothing stays the same. Those stories we talked about on Christmas night, they're important for your kids, they're part of their heritage, but they also belong to the past. The world changes, the stories change."

Language alive because it can die. The word made flesh so eternity is an unwelcome gift to it. There was a time when my parents' lives must also have felt as though they were always in flux, always moving, until gradually the years came and went and became a sequence of waiting. Is what I sometimes perceive as apathy in my father the realization that his past can no longer impel, the future pulling everything to itself? I'm relieved when, with a spark of the old spite, he shouts over his shoulder as he gets into the car, "*N'oubliez surtout pas de pratiquer votre français, les enfants. Toé aussi Kaki.*"

Geoffrey and the children are watching a hockey game and I've joined them in the den. I must look like my mother, peering over my glasses at the television screen while working on a tapestry for the seat of an old chair that's been in Geoffrey's family since he was a boy. My mother gave me the tapestry kit as a Christmas present because I'd been meaning to recover the chair for such a long time. The kit has a pattern already stamped on the webbing, but I've decided to make up my own pattern as I go along. I can imagine my mother shaking her head, saying, *ah ma belle rebelle*. I like the new configuration emerging against the stamped design.

Christine has been phoning me, urging me to go to Paris in the spring at the end of the school term. I had planned to go to Montreal for a few months, be by myself for a while, but she's insisting that I go to Paris instead. Rent a studio for a few months, give myself a gift, a block of time for writing. Madame Wickersham was right, I should never have gone into teaching. After discussing the possibility with Christine, I brought out the articles Madame gave me at my graduation. I've done this so many times over the years.

Madame Wickersham was the only one ever to say that I could write, the only one to acknowledge that it was possible to be a writer even if you came from a small town in Northern Ontario. "Gather your stories, your diaries, your fragments, your dictionary definitions, and put them into a book," she would advise, as casually as if it were truly possible. As if a young girl from Ansonville, from the other side of the tracks from Iroquois Falls, could truly become a writer. But then Christine did it, she became an artist. Why couldn't I become a writer?

Going to Paris to write seems such a worn-out cliché, belonging to another age, but it also makes the possibility more feasible somehow. Time to throw caution to the wind, Christine says, time to let down my guard. Visit museums, art shows, immerse myself in everything French, maybe try my hand at writing in my mother tongue, unconstrained by rules, family, expectations. Not that Paris offers superior models, it's just different, Christine says. The dispossession of being elsewhere offers different perspectives, forces you to think differently.

Louise and David are old enough to look after themselves, and in any event Geoffrey will be here with them. They are actually quite enthusiastic at the idea. The thought of their mother acquiring some of Christine's refinement. Still, I feel guilty just thinking about the possibility of leaving them, if only for a few months.

Louise is cheering louder than her brother and father, excited more by the prospect of winning a bet than by a goal scored by the Canadiens. This is probably her way of letting me know that she's not above allying herself with her grandparents, or me, at least for a few hours. And it's also her way of allying herself with her brother and father. In betting against the team they are cheering for, she has acknowledged their interest in the game, if only for one night. It's the kind of alliance that's more enduring than teams. It's the kind of alliance that will not be reduced to strategies of antagonism.

LE BAISER DE JUAN-LES-PINS

Il pleut. . . . The various greys of the roofs and sky are the usual greys one reads about in books on Paris, the cobblestone streets a perfect setting for a Renoir film where almost every shot begins with someone exiting or entering a frame, leaving several frames in between empty. It has rained almost every day since I arrived a month ago; the studio is dank with the breath of old velvet furniture and drapes. I've returned to Paris wanting to write but too much time is spent gazing out windows or reading about France in France, and not enough time writing what should be written. I'd been under the impression that I'd be able to gather my notes into stories here, but the moment I put pen to paper the stories empty themselves of all content, as if I've become inaccessible to myself.

I've never been to Christine's studio and I haven't seen her since she left Canada in March so I look forward to our visit this morning. Her studio is on rue Villiers de l'Isle-Adam, a name I came across last night in *Flaubert's Parrot.* Only the French would designate a short street after an obscure writer. My own studio is on rue Edouard Vaillant near Levallois. Who were these men?

Christine is working on an installation for an upcoming

show: six tall diptychs the size of French windows. Half of them are black-and-white photographs three feet wide and eight feet high. Some are details of a classic Roman Venus taken from different angles, others are shots of streets lined with tombs. She has paired each of these six photographs with either a framed sheet of stainless steel or a sheet of lead in the same dimensions, and hung them on walls painted midnight blue. The various greys of the photographs, the stainless steel, and the lead stand out like narrow windows against the midnight wall. The lead panels, she explains, are inert surfaces that reflect nothing, but when I walk past the stainless steel panels, shadows stir against their surface. Beside the static images of the past, the stainless panels offer blurred reflections of the present.

Christine's studio is just around the corner from Père Lachaise, so after lunch we stroll through the hush of the cemetery, where she took several of the photographs. As we track down Colette, Bernhardt, Proust, Apollinaire, she explains how her diptychs play out the relation between image and object, between past and present. Her photographs of the tombs, which idealize, encapsulate the history of the body's decay, are records of the mortal remains, she says. The dead evoked by monuments marked by their name. We look for Beauvoir and Sartre but can't find them. Who decides who will be buried at Lachaise?

Christine wants to spend the rest of the afternoon working on the installation so we make plans to meet later for the evening performance of Roman Polanski's interpretation of Gregor Samsa, "in honour of Madame Wickersham". I should have kept in touch with her, I could have sent her a postcard to let her know that her illicit guidance was not all in vain, but she's probably dead by now.

As I wend my way towards Place des Vosges, past Victor Hugo's house, I'm reminded of the extravagant musical about to open in Toronto. Les Miz. The irony of having his words adapted to accordions and kettledrums in spite of his steadfast hatred of music. I stop at the Bibliothèque Historique, spend an hour in the reading room with its magnificent ceiling, scrutinize original manuscripts, our most reliable witnesses to our literary past. I then walk towards Hôtel Salé, which is now the Musée Picasso.

The viewing starts on the first floor with Picasso's famous "Self-Portrait from the Blue Period". He is muffled in a black coat against a blue background, his gaze both disillusioned and passionate. The allegorical starting point.

The layout of the museum is such that twenty rooms represent different periods: Blue, Rose, Cubist, Classic, Avignon, Guernica. . . . Biographical information and photographs grace the entrance of each room, as if to better tally the movement of time, like a family album. Picasso at seven with his sister Lola. A note in his handwriting at the bottom of the photograph states that her dress is black with a blue sash and white collar and his suit is white with a navy-blue overcoat and a blue beret. The writing rounds out the details that faded sepia can't convey.

Snapshots of special events—Picasso as a matador at a ball, meetings with friends, wives, lovers, children—take on mythical proportions as most viewers spend more time inspecting the photographs and biographical details than they do looking at the paintings. There's more interest in what can be translated into certainty.

By the time I reach Mougins, the last years, the

drizzle outside has flourished into a downpour. Two hours still before meeting Christine, so I retrace my steps from the erotic drawings of Picasso's old age. Are these the evidence of an old man's obsession, or the aesthetic affirmation of a vibrant life? I search early paintings of women for an answer, especially those that follow the first bloom of infatuation, but in their fashionable abstract configurations the women no longer speak for themselves. As if each one had been discharged from who she was and condemned to the puerility of the artist's dreams.

Polanski is brilliant. As Samsa awakens to his nightmare world, the transformation from man to insect is not as discernible on stage as on the shadow projected on the backdrop. It would have been too contrived to alter his appearance with makeup or costumes, and what the audience sees as the subtle changes of his body lying on the bed or crawling on the floor is projected as slowly evolving deformations by Samsa's shadow. The other realm through which we imagine our other selves. There are at least a dozen curtain calls and Polanski receives a standing ovation. This is what I came to Paris for.

After the performance, Christine suggests a late dinner at a Moroccan restaurant in Le Marais, but when we get there the owner informs us he's closing up. "But my friend came all the way from Canada just to eat here," Christine protests, and her exaggerated disappointment extracts an invitation to join the owner, his family, and a few friends for dinner, as long as we don't mind couscous. He's always liked Canadians, he concedes, and the evening promises to be an animated occasion in spite of a young Frenchman dressed as what is best described as a walking piece of art. In a tone drenched with hauteur he declares, as he retreats towards the exit, that he intensely dislikes Canadians, "Ils sont comme les boches," the owner hollering after him, "Quel caractère de cochon!" Like Giraudoux, their favourite playwright, many French still equate foreigners with fleas on a dog, a menace to their spirit of perfection. "I guess it's not camp to be Canadian," Christine whispers, and laughs.

The couscous is the best I've ever tasted, the large mutton bones filled with marrow we scoop out and spread on chunks of crusty bread. Our hosts seem delighted to learn that Christine is an artist and that I, according to Christine, am a writer. "If you were stranded on an island and had the choice of one book to take with you, one book to teach you about the world and yourself, which would you choose?" someone asks. "My own," I counter, not admitting to the fact that I haven't written one yet, and the evening progresses through loud debates and louder songs until well past two in the morning.

Because it's too late for the Métro and the restaurant owner has refused to "accept Canadian money", Christine and I decide to splurge on separate taxis. Fortified by wine, cognac, and earnest resolutions to set to work first thing in the morning we walk towards a taxi stand near La Bastille. The procedure requires that we hire the car at the head of the line so I ask the peculiar-looking man leaning against the first car if he will take me to Levallois. As he opens the rear door I notice he's very short, the top of his head barely reaching my shoulders. Not exactly a midget, but his proportions are all wrong and his head, too large for his body, is haloed by a mane of long white hair jutting out like that of a hooded capuchin monkey. He reminds me of a circus attraction.

No sooner have I settled into the seclusion of the

back seat than the driver turns around to inspect me and I'm struck with the error of my choice. It's almost three a.m. and I'm driving through the deserted streets of Paris with a monkey who keeps turning to gawk. Part of me cautions that I should get out at the next red light, but another part argues that I'm paranoid.

"How long have you driven a cab?" Twenty years confirms my paranoia. He turns again and stares. I'm compelled to strike some kind of conversation if only as a precautionary measure.

"You have an accent, are you Spanish?"

"Portuguese, but I've lived here many years. And you, you're not French."

"Canadian," I reply.

"Ah! I wouldn't have guessed it. Swedish, Swiss perhaps, but not Canadian. You don't speak French with a Canadian accent."

"I speak French in many languages," I reply.

The answer seems to surprise him and he turns around as if to confirm a first impression. He stares. The features of his face are dissonant, none co-operate, and I realize that my apprehension is due more to his appearance than to the fact that he keeps taking his eyes off the road.

"Are you married?" Yes.

"Is your husband here with you?"

"Yes," I lie, and to justify the folly of a woman on her own so late at night I add, "I wasn't alone, I was with friends." This odious little man bores me. Why should I explain myself to a taxi driver? I will definitely make a quick exit at the next red light.

"It's impossible to get taxis around here at this time of night." The monkey reads minds. When he twists his body to look back again, I realize it's because he's too short for his rearview mirror. Those very people you would prefer to be invisible are always those who think they have the right to connect with you eye to eye. When my husband and I lived here, it took me months to learn how to glaze my focus and walk past beggars or ogling men. As if they didn't exist.

"I said it's impossible to get taxis at this time." Indifference makes the monkey belligerent.

"There are over 15,000 taxis crawling the sewers of this city day and night." The reference to sewers should generate the appropriate association. He looks like a rat, and sooner or later you have to play the game according to the rules of this predatory city. And the rules require that you begin with those who are clearly at a disadvantage.

After a few moments' silence, he leans towards the passenger seat and retrieves two pillows on which he perches to receive a better image through his mirror. I dismiss him with a sneer and turn my head towards the darkness on my right. The sky is the same inert grey as Christine's lead panels.

With the monkey's eyes fastened on me I feel the distance I need beginning to dissolve. I am confined to the space of a mirror framing his dark eyes and the bushy eyebrows that slant and meet on the bridge of his misshapen nose. I am visited by a wretched face that holds me hostage to its wretchedness.

"It amuses madame perhaps that I'm so short?"

"Yes." Some shortcomings are such that you can only react with callousness.

"And that I'm ugly, madame finds it amusing or offensive?"

"At the moment, I find it neither amusing nor offensive. If anything I find it rather tedious. Your fate has nothing to do with me."

"On the contrary, madame, your fate may have a lot to do with me."

There are moments, fleeting seconds during the course of an event, when the outcome of your next word or action balances by such a thin thread that your heart stops for the duration of several beats. One altered breath would upset that balance. My eyes lift to the mirror and meet his. The light behind their disillusionment is not unfamiliar.

"But madame may leave if she wishes." He stops the car.

"I'm very tired. Just take me home. Please." The last word a precautionary whisper.

To get to Pont Levallois from La Bastille, it is necessary to cross the entire city from the southeast to the northwest, and I'm astounded to discover that in spite of fifteen minutes in the cab we haven't crossed the city at all. We are travelling along Jean Jaurès on the northeastern side of Paris. My friend Guansé has a studio on this street, so I know it well.

"Why are we still going north instead of west?" I ask.

"It is much quicker at this time to cross the city along the Boulevard, madame."

"I have a friend who lives on this street, perhaps I should stop here."

"As you wish, madame." Again he stops the car.

We are at least fifteen blocks from Guansé's studio and I don't even know if he's home. "No. No, there's no point in waking him up at this time. Go on."

The mirror stares. "What does he do, this friend who lives on this street?"

"He's an artist. Catalan." In France, Spain isn't so

different from Portugal, and surely he wouldn't hurt someone who has a friend who's both a foreigner and a Catalan.

"Ah yes, the French love artists, especially if they're Catalan. Unfortunately, they don't feel the same about foreign taxi drivers," the mirror says.

"They don't feel the same about most foreigners," I reply and the mirror smiles. In France, the foreigner's only friends are foreigners.

"What about madame, how does she feel about them?"

"Who? Artists, foreigners, or taxi drivers?"

"All of them, madame."

"I like some artists. I seldom think of people as foreigners and I don't really know any taxi drivers."

"But madame knows many artists. I would bet madame knows many live ones as well as dead ones. She comes to Paris to visit museums."

I am relieved we are finally on the Boulevard Périphérique, travelling west towards Levallois. The conversation threatens to veer towards the privileged artist versus the underprivileged cab driver and I'm in no mood for social criticism. He's setting me up for a large tip which I will gladly pay if I ever make it home.

"You know why I drive a cab at night?" he continues. "It's because I've had it up to here driving damn tourists to and from museums. People are nicer at night when they've been eating and drinking. I would wager madame went to a museum today."

It's a wager that I concede with pleasure. "Yes. Musée Picasso."

"Ah, Picasso! And did madame enjoy it? Does madame find Picasso's paintings beautiful?" The mirror will not give up.

"Art isn't necessarily beautiful. Picasso's shapes are compositions, metaphors for larger ranges of experience." Why am I speaking to this monkey about art?

"Larger than what, madame?"

"Larger than what we usually experience, I suppose." Under the yellow lights of the Boulevard, against space as blank as a monitor, red traces of tail-lights sweep by.

"Most of my passengers tell me his paintings are abstract. So they don't have to tell me what they mean," he continues, the perfect model of persistence.

"Because you have this conversation with most of your passengers," I retaliate with a sarcastic upper hand. It is my turn to glare at the mirror. His eyes are no longer staring, no longer steady or merely curious. They shift from side to side in search of an image beyond the mirror's surface. "Do you think his bodies are abstract?" he asks.

"It depends on the period. Some are abstract."

"Can madame define for me the value of an abstract body?" His tone a challenge that can't be dismissed.

"I suppose it resides in its form and is independent of the subject of the painting. It has nothing to do with meaning or with the body painted, but with lines, colours, and surfaces. The subject can't be compared to other subjects but exists through its form."

The mirror is broad with a distorted smile. "Bravo, madame. You are the first passenger to give me such an eloquent answer. Is madame an artist?" His voice is filled with scorn.

"A writer." My reaction, urgent, wants to dissociate itself from his branding.

We have taken the exit at Porte Champerret, a few minutes from rue Édouard Vaillant, and I'm relieved that the conversation can finally come to an end. He's not a violent man but my indifference is being eroded. There are circuitous ways of breaking into a person's isolation and the monkey is proving to be a master. The meter registers 120 francs, not surprising considering his roundabout route, but there's no point complaining at this stage. When he stops a few doors from my building, I hand him 200 francs and ask for 60 francs change.

My arm holding the money is extended over the front seat while he looks through his wallet. He is stalling and I expect him to say he doesn't have the proper change when suddenly he seizes my forearm and yanks it with such force that I assume he wants to drag me into the front seat. Within a few seconds, however, he has pulled himself over the front seat using my arm as a lever and he is half sitting, half lying across me in the back. I hold onto my briefcase with my left arm while trying to open the door on my right but his grip prevents me from reaching the handle. His hand is enormous, disproportionate to the length of his arm, and pawlike, the fingers short and stubby.

"You can let go of your purse, I don't want your damn money."

"What do you want then?"

"I want you to sit here for a few more minutes and talk to me. You needn't be afraid, I won't hurt you."

"You're hurting me now. Let go of my arm."

He loosens his grip and orders me to face him. "Tell me, if I were a Picasso invention would you find me interesting? Would you spend hours before me figuring out why my nose is flat, my nostrils so dilated? How would you interpret a chin that juts too much to one side and legs that are so short and bandy?"

His face is only a few inches away from mine, his teeth in a state of advanced decay, his breath oppressive. Our eyes have locked, his waiting for an answer, mine hoping he will find it without my having to speak it. But my silence makes him impatient. "*Tu réponds, non?*"

"You already know the answer," I mutter.

"You find me disgusting."

"If you stalk all your clients to ask them if they find you disgusting, you must have your answer by now."

"I want *your* answer," he shouts, clenching my arm. "Do you find me disgusting?"

"Yes."

"But you don't find Picasso's bodies disgusting, merely abstract." As he speaks, his left arm enlaces my neck while his right hand slowly slips from my arm to my shoulder. The flat of his palm glides down my chest, stops at my breast. The cotton of my blouse and the lace of my brassiere grate gently back and forth against my nipple. I am wedged in his vice-like grip against the car seat, my feet dangling halfway to the floor, unable to regain a foothold. His smile exposes more rotting teeth and as he kisses me, his target eye hovering above mine, my mouth fills with the taste of fermented decay. I am paralysed with repugnance and fear.

After a long and astonishingly tender kiss, he begins to trace with his tongue a slow path along my jawline, inside my ear, down the side of my neck to my collarbone, into the opening of my blouse. As his mouth searches, reaches a nipple, I'm startled by the convulsive turbulence invading me. A warm sensation shoots to the pit of my stomach, explodes inside my groin. I'm horrified. This reaction is banned, taboo, transgresses everything I know to be right. Yet the sensation has assumed the force of an unknown, unnamed law that possesses me so completely that it divests me of who I am. Who I thought I was.

"Please, let me go."

His tongue slowly retraces its path. "Very well, madame," and without the slightest hesitation he releases his grip, delves into his pocket, hands me sixty francs change. "Bonsoir, madame," his tone casual, with no hint of apology.

As soon as I reach the studio I rush to the bathroom and stand before the mirror as if to corroborate what has just happened. Explain or at least tame my unexpected reaction. Except for a long trace of spittle running from my jawbone to the opening of my blouse, the mirror tells me nothing. His saliva. I scrub my neck, rinse my mouth, brush my teeth, but still the taste of decay lingers and his face keeps appearing like a visitation.

Unable to sleep, I retrieve from my briefcase the guide to the Picasso Museum, flip through it until an image dated 1925 lunges at me. In an explosion of garish colours, two intertwining bodies kiss, their limbs and organs so topsy-turvy it's impossible to tell which ones belong to the man and which to the woman. Each detail—a mouth which could also be an eye or female genitals, a phallic nose, a corrugated cardboard foot—is part of a puzzle whose pieces have been scattered in order to bind the two figures in a passionate but violent embrace. The commentary beside the image states, "Art is never chaste."

I pick up my pen and on the first page of the French scribbler I bought more than a month ago, I begin to write. *Le baiser de Juan-Les-Pins. It was raining. . . .*

THE CHORUS (iii)

frogs that have weathered several glacial periods
will somehow or other get through this one too.
remember eh. those frogs.

Kusano Shimpei
frogs &. others.

To this day I associate the fragrance of lilac with a feeling of impending freedom. The flowering bushes that lined the fence around the convent grounds throughout the month of June meant escape. In a few days, a few weeks, the voices of parents in the *parloir* would reach study hall and the fragrance of lilac would be displaced by other familiar perfumes: a handkerchief stored among gauzy packets of dried flowers and leaves, the scent of hands and hair washed with the turquoise contents of a bottle by a washbasin. Each year in the month of June, in a lilac branch, a childhood hides. Each year in the month of June, in a lilac branch, a childhood is set free.

It isn't always the same childhood. Memory has a way of building different rooms in which to lodge itself. A chapel where the scent of incense and melting wax blends with the lilacs that crowd the altar in celebration of the feast of Saint Joan, who also heeded heavenly voices. Dressed in her suit of armour, riding wherever the Archangel Michael directed her. There is also a convent dormitory, a small bedroom overlooking the parking lot of the Union Hotel, the porch framing two sides of a cottage where I used to read my way through the heroes and heroines of Junior Classics—child of the sea made knight, or the fair princess Micomicona who was transformed into Dorothea.

After six weeks in Paris I decided to spend the rest of the summer at my parents' cottage. Paris has only confirmed that I don't belong there either. In any event it proved to be too distracting, with all its museums and art, although I did manage to write the beginning of a story there. What I need now is the isolation and quiet of Northern Ontario, my old home ground, especially since this will be my last time here. My parents retired here after they sold the hotel, built a permanent home beside the original cottage, which then became a summer place for myself and my family. But now that my father isn't well the property is too much work and too isolated for them, so they have to sell it.

I'm going to miss coming here. Geoffrey and the children will join me in a few days and I look forward to seeing them, although now that I'm writing every day I like the time by myself as well. I've moved my writing table by the windows overlooking the bay and I get up early each morning, when the lake looks like a clean slate. The lilac bushes my mother planted at the corner of the cottage waver like the heads of elderly ladies striving to keep the mannered elegance of their youth. June Lilac. Wickersham.

I had planned to write a novel about an old woman looking back on her life, in the hope, I suppose, that old age would reveal its secrets. I had even imagined her death. "Next Sunday after my funeral, Christine and I will go for our walk as we always do. . . ." I had thought the future no more difficult to invent than the past, but as in the story "The Old Woman and the Knight," the crone keeps transforming herself into a young girl. Through the telling of stories the body reproduces itself.

My first memory is of my mother and my father telling stories, when years went by like turtles, but now the years jump around like the proverbial hare. I am a middle-aged woman whose phantom body of old age hovers and dreams of the agility of its youth. The long back legs of the frog that leaps twenty times the length of its body. The frog mouth that lodges for days and weeks its unhatched eggs, its unclean spirits. The long tongue that shoots out and captures everything in its path. The frog yearns to change its skin, pull it over its head like a dress, place it in its mouth, chew it, ingest it, so the fiction of that body is never lost.

The young girl dressed in black: black stockings, black tunic with crisp white collar and cuffs, her fine blonde hair awkwardly cut. Head bent over a book, she's cramming for a science test in spite of the nun's warnings that cramming will only make her forget everything right after the test. But she didn't forget, because as I look across the bay I remember how the movement of heat converts into new forms of energy as it travels from one place to the next. I remember a diagram of a blue ball and a red ball chasing each other in orbit, each one careful not to collide for fear she'll annihilate each other. I remember how each has an electric charge of opposite polarity, the same particle reversed in time.

Strange what the mind chooses to remember. It's very quiet here at night, except for the occasional loon, and frogs singing at a silken moon, their song rising, rising. I hardly notice them unless they fall silent, as one misses the ticking of a clock when it stops.

Every day between six o'clock in the morning and ten o'clock at night a church bell across the lake rings the hours, a sound one almost never hears any more. Although I haven't set foot in a church in years, except for concerts, I prefer its bells to the talking clock the children gave me last Christmas. It speaks French. They thought it would be a fitting present since hardly anyone speaks French to me now. *Il est six heures*, the flat nasal tone of its computer voice whines every morning. *Il est sept heures*, it nags an hour later, and when it doesn't speak, its green turquoise hour glares at me throughout the night. A clock without an hour hand robs you of the impression that time moves in cycles. Without the large wheels attached to the small toothed wheel, it's impossible to imagine the earth rotating on its axis among the stars.

At an oversized table in study hall, the young girl examines an old and elaborate instrument that displays the movements of the planets around the sun. In the centre of the instrument there is a large brass ball around which the three innermost planets, Mercury, Venus, and Earth, revolve. The universe was smaller then. When she turns the handle attached to the brass ball, an ingenious system of gears causes the planets to rotate around the sun in their relative positions while the moon moves in its orbit around the earth. The apparatus, attached to a large circular disk, divides the calendar into twelve months, each division revealing the different affections of the planets and the signs of the zodiac. In the blue sections between the planets, the pale outlines of angels hold scrolls too faded to decipher.

The angels are very important to her. They watch over her when she leaves the convent for holidays or when she crosses a street to avoid walking past boys or dogs. They watch over her when she returns to the convent and has to sit in the corner. That's why, whenever she can, she wears a black tam. It's because of the angels. So their wings won't get caught in her fine blonde hair.

"Who's your favourite angel? Michael or Gabriel?" Christine used to ask at the *pensionnat.*

"Gabriel," the young girl said then. *L'Ange du Seigneur annonça à Marie.* Words of an angel made flesh, *la chair,* but now all angels are equally important, no matter what name we give them. It is angels that put faces and names to everything invisible and strange. *L'étrange. L'être-ange.* My grandmothers. The *loup-garou.* The iron horse. Baby boa. Kaki.

After gathering several stories about the young girl's past, I have just finished the story I began in Paris about a woman and a taxi driver. "Le Baiser de Juan-les-Pins." I tried writing it in French but had to retreat once again to English. Had to concede that most of my writing will be in English, everything transformed as if to free itself from the constraints of allegiances and convent walls. I'm not proud of it, but there is no time left for guilt or remorse.

The story from Paris is a curious one that I haven't quite deciphered yet, except perhaps as a demarcation between the past, that other room that is always resisting closure, and the future. Between the young girl and myself.

Kaki. She liked to play grown-up with her mother's makeup. Smear her face with powder and kohl, outline her lips in carmine red, the colours marking the crossing of a boundary between the imaginary world of childhood and a time when she would speak in her own name. A ceremony marking the slow progression towards the day when she would transform the "Princess of the Frogs" into the teller of her own stories.

ACKNOWLEDGMENTS

Frog Moon is a novel whose characters are fictional; however, I would like to extend my gratitude to all pioneer voices that form the basis of its historical, legendary, and mythological chronology, especially my parents, Laurette and Achilles Lemire; also to the gatherers of French Canadian myths, Claude Aubry, Marius Barbeau, Philippe-Aubert de Gaspé; the Algonquin and Cree people for their sacred legend of Oma-ka-ki-geesis; Junior Classics, Collier & Son; L'Encyclopédie de la Jeunesse, Grolier; the contributors of *Maclean's* during the magazine's early years, especially Mr. Woollacott and the anonymous schoolmarm; *Gray's Anatomy*; Christine Davis, and the many women writers and theorists to whom I owe so much.

My deep appreciation to Jerry Tostevin and Smaro Kamboureli.

I would also like to extend my thanks to Frank Davey, Jan Geddes, and Gena Gorrell for their editorial suggestions, and to the Canada Council and the Ontario Arts Council for their financial support.